ll "Oṃ Namaḥ Pārvatī Pataye Hara Hara Mahādeva" ll

30 days to my Suicide

~

every choice matters

"A journey through despair, hope, and the courage to survive."

Dr. Pankaj Srivastava

Shivoham

Culture! Literature! Creation!

Shivoham

Culture! Literature! Creation!

An Imprint of Om Research Center (Publisher)

SA 17/3, P-4, Sri Krishna Nagar, Paharia

Ghazipur Road, Varanasi, Uttar Pradesh, India. Pin-221007

Phone: +915422586191 Mobile: +919305861009

E-mail: shivohamvaranasi@gmail.com

30 days to my Suicide ~ every choice matters

ISBN: 978-81-982619-3-9

First Edition 2025

Disclaimer

This is a work of fiction. Names, characters, organizations, places, events, and incidents are either products of the author's imagination or are used fictitiously. Any resemblance to actual persons, living or dead, or actual events is purely coincidental.

"30 Days to My Suicide: Every Choice Matters" contains themes related to mental health, depression, trauma, and suicide. These subjects are depicted solely for the purpose of creative expression and storytelling. The author does not intend to encourage, promote, or romanticize self-harm, suicide, or any form of mental distress.

Readers are advised to approach this book with discretion. If you or someone you know is experiencing emotional distress, depression, or thoughts of self-harm, please reach out for help immediately. You are not alone.

In India, you can contact:

National Tele Mental Programme of India (Tele Manas):

14416 OR 1800-891-4416.

https://telemanas.mohfw.gov.in/home

For readers outside India, please contact your local mental health helpline or seek support from a licensed professional. Every life has value. Every choice matters — including the choice to reach out for help.

Dedicated

To

My patients, past and present,

Who taught me that pain speaks softly

And that healing begins when

Someone truly listens.

Your story matters !

Your life matters !!

You matter !!!

Preface

"We must accept finite disappointment, but never lose infinite hope." — Martin Luther King, Jr.

If you are holding this book right now, chances are you are searching—for answers, for hope, or maybe just for someone who understands the weight you're carrying. I don't know your story, but I want to begin by saying this: you are not alone.

As a doctor, I have spent countless hours listening to people's stories—not just the medical facts, but the unspoken pain behind their eyes, the hesitation in their voices, the weight in their silences. Healing is not always about stitches, medicines, or scans. Sometimes, the deepest wounds are invisible—the ones carried quietly in the mind and the heart.

Over the years, I have met patients, students, and young people who confessed their struggles only in whispers, often after gathering every ounce of courage. Many admitted that they had thought of giving up. Some had even tried. They did not lack intelligence, opportunities, or even love. What they lacked, most painfully, was hope. And this is not rare. According to the World Health Organization (WHO), nearly 800,000 people die by suicide every year—that's one life lost every 40 seconds.

For every death, there are many more attempts, and countless silent struggles that never reach the surface. Among young people aged 15–29, suicide is one of the leading causes of death worldwide. These are not just statistics. Each number is a story, a family, a circle of friends left with unanswered questions. Each represents someone who felt cornered by pain, unable to see another way forward.

Suicide is not just a personal tragedy—it is a silent epidemic that touches families, schools, workplaces, and societies. Yet, we hesitate to speak about it. We cover it in shame, in fear, in silence. And in that silence, countless lives are lost.

That is why I chose this subject. Not because it is easy—it is not. Not because it is comfortable—it is far from it. But because it is necessary. Because every day that we don't talk about it, someone suffers alone, believing they have no way out.

Why a story? Because sometimes, advice feels heavy. But a story feels like a friend. A friend who doesn't preach, but simply sits beside you and whispers, "I've been there too."

This book is my attempt to start that conversation in a way that is human, relatable, and safe. Rather than presenting only statistics or clinical terms, I wanted to tell a story—a story that feels like a mirror for those who are struggling, and like a window for those who want to understand.

Aarav's journey in this novel is fictional, but his thoughts and emotions are drawn from the very real stories I've witnessed as a doctor, and sometimes even as a fellow human being walking through life's storms. His 30-day countdown is not about glorifying despair—it is about exploring it honestly, and then finding the fragile threads of courage that can turn despair into resilience.

And if you are a parent, teacher, or caregiver reading this, I want you to know that this book is also for you. Too often, adults misinterpret silence as strength, or dismiss withdrawal as a phase. But sometimes, silence is a scream. Sometimes, withdrawal is a warning. Through Aarav's journey, I hope you will gain insight into the quiet battles so many young people fight. Your understanding, patience, and compassion may be the very lifeline someone needs.

I wrote this because I believe stories heal. When a struggling young person sees themselves in Aarav, they may feel less alone. When a friend, parent, or teacher reads his journey, they may better understand how to extend compassion instead of judgment. And when society begins to see suicide not as a shameful secret but as a cry for help, perhaps we can save lives—quietly, one by one.

If you are reading this, I hope you will walk with Aarav through these 30 days, not as a passive reader but as someone who carries the message forward: that no life is too broken to heal, no mind too lost to find peace, and no darkness too deep for a spark of hope to enter.

If you've ever asked yourself, "Why should I keep going? Why should I not just end it?" then this book is my hand reaching out to you, saying: "Read one day at a time. Walk with Aarav. And maybe, just maybe, you'll find a reason to stay."

This is more than a book. It is an invitation—to speak, to listen, and to believe that every tomorrow is worth living for. Let us walk together through these 30 days—not as strangers, but as fellow travelers—toward an array of hope.

With empathy and conviction,
Dr. Pankaj Srivastava

I will defend the importance of bedtime stories to my last gasp. —JK Rowling

---

Note to Readers: My true friends..!!

"Do one thing every day that scares you." —Eleanor Roosevelt

Hey Friends!,

If you've opened this book, it probably means you're going through something heavy—or maybe you're just curious. Either way, I want to start by telling you something most people forget to say out loud: "Your feelings are real. Your pain is valid. And you matter."

This book isn't here to judge you. It's not here to give you cheesy motivational lines or make fake promises. Instead, it's here to walk with you—day by day, thought by thought—through the life of a boy named Aarav who once felt exactly like you might feel now. He thought he was done with life. But in 30 days, through tears, doubts, tiny sparks of joy, and unexpected moments of courage, he discovered that hope doesn't arrive in a big, magical way. It comes quietly, in small choices.

I don't know what tomorrow looks like for you. But I do know this: if you give yourself one more day, and then another, life has a way of surprising you. And you deserve to see those surprises.

So, as you read Aarav's story, treat it like a mirror. Let it reflect your fears, your doubts, and your possibilities. You don't have to relate to everything. But maybe one scene, one line, one thought will stick with you—and become the reason you keep going. We'll take this slowly, one day at a time. And now: you're not alone anymore.

Your friend,
Pankaj
Love You!!

Milestones

Acknowledgments

To my wife, Dr. Shalini Srivastava –
you are the heartbeat behind every word I write and the calm within every storm I face.

This book is as much yours as it is mine, for your love has been the quiet fire that kept my spirit alive through sleepless nights and uncertain thoughts.

In your presence, I find peace; in your eyes, I find purpose. You believed in me when silence was my only voice, and your faith became the bridge between my dreams and their becoming.

If these pages carry any truth, any tenderness, or any light – it is because of you.

I also extend my heartfelt thanks to all those who have walked beside me – family, friends, readers, and well-wishers – whose subtle encouragement and kind words have shaped both the writer and the human within me.

To all who read these pages with empathy – you complete this journey.

Forever grateful,
Pankaj

Day-1: The Decision

"The heaviest burdens are the ones we carry in silence."

The clock flushed 12:07 a.m. in the dark, casting a dim red light across Aarav's small room. His textbooks were still scattered on the desk, but they hadn't been opened in hours. He sat on the edge of his bed, staring at the ceiling as though it held all the answers he had been searching for-and none at the same time.
Rain streaked down the windowpane, tapping a relentless rhythm against the glass. The world seemed muted, muffled, as if life itself had pressed a heavy hand over everything.

He whispered, the words trembling in his throat. The thought had been coming more often lately, like an uninvited guest who refused to leave.

"Thirty days... That's it. Thirty more days of this meaningless life, and then I'll be free." He muttered.

The thought had been spinning his head for weeks, but tonight it finally landed with a cold certainty. The notebook lay open on his desk, untouched for days. Inside were words he hadn't been able to write lately—words he didn't have the strength to face: anger, pain, hopelessness.

Why bother? He asked myself again.

He grabbed his old diary from the drawer, flipped to a blank page, and scribbled the words:

30" Days to My Suicide."

His hand trembled as he wrote it. For the first time, the plan didn't just live in his mind—it existed on paper. Something inside him both tightened and relaxed at once.

"Is this... relief? Or surrender?"

"What will happen if his plan doesn't work?' 'The mind boggles!"

Aarav let out a shaky laugh. "Maybe both."

He started taking to himself-

"You've tried enough. Failed enough. No one cares. What's the point of dragging this misery for years?"

"But... is this really the end? Do I even know what's after?"

"Anything is better than this vacuum."

"Or... maybe I just never learned how to live."

"What exactly happened, I really didn't know?

He pressed the diary to his chest. The tears didn't come, though his heart begged for the shedding. His eyes felt too dry, too heavy, as though even crying had abandoned him.

He muffled-

"Maybe they'd be better off without him."

"No one would notice anyway."

"I'm useless. I've always been useless."

The voice in his head was insistent, a shadow that followed every movement, every heartbeat. He hugged his knees tighter, feeling the cold of the wooden floor against his feet.

"Stop it, he whispered".

"Stop thinking that way."

But the thoughts didn't stop. They contained, clawed, and dragged him deeper into a place he knew too well.

His mind wandered back to a memory-

Ten-year-old Aarav running barefoot in the rain, laughing as water splashed against his legs. His mother had stood at the doorway, yelling for him to come inside before he caught a cold. His father had watched with a rare smile, clapping along as if Aarav had just won a race.

"When did that boy disappear? When did life stop feeling like rain and start feeling like drowning?"

Another instance shook his mind when he was eight years old, running across the school playground, trying to escape the dull ache of loneliness that had already begun to settle in his chest. His shoes were worn, laces fraying, but he didn't care. He just wanted to run, to feel free for a few moments.

"Look at him! His shoes are falling apart!"

The laughter hit him harder than any stone could. He tripped and fell into the dust, scraping his knees. Pain flared sharply, but it wasn't the blood that stung—it was the silence that followed. The teacher had seen, but didn't intervene.

He uttered-

"I remembered looking around, seeing the other children playing, laughing, belonging. And me... I was nothing."

"Why am I so small in everyone else's world?"

That question had never left him.

He was trying to come out of these thoughts, but suddenly screamed to remember another event that had dug him too deep. At thirteen, he sat at the dinner table, spoon hovering over his plate. His father slammed his hand down.

"Why are your grades so low again, Aarav? Do you even try?"

"I—I tried, Papa..." he stammered, but his father didn't hear him.

"Don't lie! Your cousin got ninety-five, and you—worthless! Useless!" His father shouted.

My mother said nothing. She stood by the kitchen doorway, silent, her eyes averted.

That night, he hid in his room, staring at the ceiling, nails digging into his arms, asking the same impossible question: Why am I still here?

The Dilemma begins in his mind and he flipped to a new page and began listing reasons:

Reasons to Die (...muttering)

"I'm a failure."

"No one understands me."

"I'm tired of pretending."

"Life is pointless."

Reasons to Live (...smiled and down the pen)

The second list remained empty. He tapped the pen against the paper, waiting for a thought, a whisper, anything. Nothing came.

"See? Not a single reason. It's over."

He rubbed his temples, feeling the tension, the ache that seemed to radiate from his chest to his fingertips. He felt invisible, insignificant, unworthy. And yet... he was still alive. He didn't know why?

Maybe it's fear, he thought. Fear of the unknown. Fear of leaving everything behind.

Or maybe... maybe it was something else. A small, stubborn spark buried somewhere inside him, refusing to die.

He picked up the diary finally, fingers trembling. For a long while, nothing came. Then, slowly, words started to spill-

"I feel empty."

"I feel lost."

“I feel like I’m drowning in a place where no one notices me.”

Tears came quietly at first, then in a torrent. I pressed my face to the pillow, letting the sobs shake me, letting the pain exist without pretending it didn’t.

He closed the diary and whispered aloud, as though making a contract with himself:

"Thirty days, Aarav.”

“Thirty days my dear. Only Thirty days to the end."

As the night deepened, he turned off the lights and lay back in bed. The silence was deafening, broken only by the hum of the ceiling fan. His chest rose and fell, heavy with exhaustion.

For the first time in weeks, he felt a strange kind of calm—like the calm before a storm.

"Tomorrow begins the countdown," he thought. “Tomorrow, I start living my last 30 days.”

But somewhere, buried so deep even Aarav didn’t notice, a faint voice lingered:

“Or maybe... your first.”

“Even naming your pain is the first act of courage.”

Day 2 – Sleepless Nights

"Sometimes, the smallest crack lets in the most light."

The clock read 2:30 a.m. Aarav hadn't slept a minute. His room was a cage—walls closing in, silence suffocating him. He kept tossing from one side to another, staring at the ceiling, then at the shadows crawling across the corners.

"Why does night feel heavier than day?" he whispered into the emptiness.

He pressed the pillow over his head, hoping to drown out his thoughts, but the noise wasn't outside. It was inside him.

His conscious knocked –

"Why wait 30 days? Do it tonight. End it now. Who would even notice?"

"But I promised myself. 30 days... I need to see if anything changes."

"Nothing will. You've tried before. You'll fail again."

“Maybe... but what if I just want to be sure? What if I want to leave knowing I gave life one last chance?”

The dialogue in his head spun like a wheel, faster and faster. His chest tightened. He sat up, grabbing his diary from the table.

He opened to yesterday’s list. The page stared back at him:

Reasons to Die – filled.
Reasons to Live – empty.

"Pathetic," he muttered, tracing the empty lines with his pen.

Suddenly, he remembered being twelve, curled up under the blanket during a thunderstorm. His grandmother had slipped into the room, holding a lantern. She had stroked his hair and whispered, “The storm outside will pass, dear. But don’t let the storm inside grow stronger.”

Aarav blinked, a sting in his eyes.

“Storm inside... huh. Guess I lost that battle, Granny.”

The room was still dim, the only light coming from the street lamp outside the window. Shadows crawled across the walls like silent ghosts. On the bed Aarav laid still, eyes wide open, staring at the ceiling as if it could give him answers. The ceiling fan whirred slowly above, but the air felt heavy, almost suffocating.

He shook his head with the thought- “Storm inside.... What rubbish Granny is talking about?”

His heart beat fast, not from excitement but from a restless anxiety that had become his nightly companion. His hands trembled as he clutched the edge of the blanket. Sleep had abandoned him, just like, he thought, the rest of the world had.

“Why am I like this?” he whispered into the darkness. “Why can’t I do anything right?”

His voice was small, almost swallowed by the silence. He turned on his side, burying his face into the pillow, but the thoughts followed him like a tide. Everyone moves forward. Everyone achieves something. And me? Just a string of failures. Exams, friendships, even my parents’ trust—I’ve broken everything.

He felt a dull ache in his chest. The weight of the last few months sat like a stone on his heart. Rejections from college applications. Mocking words from classmates. The disappointed silence of his father at dinner. Each memory flickered like a cruel slideshow behind his eyelids.

“Maybe they’d all be happier without me,” he murmured, eyes burning. “No expectations. No shame. No me.”

A single tear slipped down his cheek. He didn’t even bother wiping it away. His mind was a battlefield: half of it whispering that it would pass, the other half urging him to escape once and for all.

What’s the point of trying again?

You’ve tried. You’ve failed. Again and again.

You’re tired. Just stop.

The clock ticked on the wall. 3:00 a.m. Time felt frozen, yet every second was unbearable. He sat up, pulling his knees to his chest, rocking slightly like a small child. His breathing came in uneven bursts. He tried to remember the last time he’d laughed. The last time someone had said, I’m proud of you. Nothing surfaced.

“Maybe tomorrow will be different,” he whispered, though he didn’t believe it. “But what if it’s not? What if it’s never different?”

He stared at his phone lying face down on the bedside table. No new messages. No calls. Just silence. The world outside slept peacefully; inside, he was drowning. His thoughts circled back to the same dark place, like a bird trapped in a cage.

It would be so easy to disappear. One step and no more noise. No more failure. Aarav shivered, not from cold but from the enormity of his own thoughts. In that moment he felt like a shadow of himself – not a boy, not a son, not a student – just a question mark floating in an endless night.

And yet, somewhere deep inside, a faint, trembling voice spoke, barely audible beneath the storm:

What if you’re wrong? What if you’re more than your failures? What if there’s still a tomorrow you can’t yet see?

He thought of something he had once read in a psychology article online:
"Sleep deprivation worsens suicidal thoughts. A tired mind cannot fight its demons."

He laughed bitterly. “No wonder my demons are winning. They never sleep. And me? I’m their favorite playground.”

At 3:45 a.m., he finally broke. A silent cry escaped his throat as tears soaked his pillow. No one heard him, no one came.

"Why does pain scream so loudly inside yet soundless outside?"

Aarav hugged himself tightly, rocking as though trying to comfort a younger version of himself. He pressed his palms to his temples, squeezing his eyes shut, trying to silence everything. But the questions stayed. And as dawn's first light crept timidly into the room, he was still awake – still caught between the weight of despair and the fragile thread of hope.

By dawn, Aarav hadn't slept a second. His eyes were swollen, his body weak, but his mind was strangely numb.

He wrote one sentence before leaving the diary open on the table:
"Another night survived. But what for?"

And then, almost as if mocking himself, he added underneath in shaky letters:

"Day 2 complete. 28 to go."

"You don't need to heal in one day; you only need to keep breathing into the next."

Day 3 – The Mask

"Your thoughts can be storms—but remember, storms always pass."

The alarm buzzed at 7:00 a.m., sharp and cruel. Aarav dragged himself out of bed, eyes swollen, body heavy from the sleepless night. He looked at the mirror, and what stared back was a ghost: pale skin, dark circles, lips cracked.

"I look like I've already died," he whispered.

But then, almost instinctively, he forced a smile. He tugged at the corners of his mouth until it resembled something human.

"There it is—the mask."

He splashed cold water on his face, combed his messy hair, and wore the mask like armor. By the time he left his room, he was no longer Aarav, the boy planning his suicide. He was just Aarav—the classmate, the friend, the son who looked "fine."

He took his bike and moved to College.

"Hey Aarav!" his friend Rahul slapped his back in the corridor. "Movie this weekend? Everyone's going!"

Aarav chuckled, the fake kind. "Yeah, sure. Count me in."

Inside, he whispered to himself: "No, you won't be there. You'll be gone in 27 days."

During class, he laughed at the teacher's jokes, nodded when friends asked for notes, and even made a sarcastic comment that earned him a round of chuckles. But under the table, his fists clenched so tight his nails dug into his palm.

He started conversation with himself

"You see how easy it is? No one notices. No one asks."

"But isn't that what you wanted? To hide?"

"No... maybe I wanted someone to look past the mask."

"At least my best friends should have predicted my mask."

"And what if they don't? What if they never do?"

He scribbled on the edge of his notebook during class:
"How loud does silence need to scream before someone hears it?"

At lunch, while pretending to enjoy his sandwich, he remembered a sports day from years ago. He had tripped in the middle of the race, knees bleeding. Everyone laughed, except his best friend Rohan, who had run back to help him up. Aarav had won nothing that day, but Rohan's words still echoed:

"Doesn't matter if you fell. What matters is—you stood up."

Now, years later, Rohan had moved away. Aarav whispered under his breath: “Wish you were here, buddy. Maybe you'd see through this mask.” Rahul broke his thoughts with laughter and said-

“Come on, bro! Cheer up, let's go to canteen for coffee”

The canteen is buzzing with chatter. Aarav sits with his friends—Rahul, Meera, Kabir. He looks calm, casual, almost carefree. But under the table, his hands fidget, nails digging into his palm.

Rahul (grinning):
"Bro, admit it—you've got some secret formula. You never look stressed and still manage good grades."

Aarav (putting on a mock-serious face):
"Ah, it's all about positive vibes, my friend. Keep calm, fake a smile, and the universe does the rest."

(The group laughs. Aarav joins, his laughter slightly louder than others, as if compensating for what he lacks inside.)

Meera (leaning in teasingly):
"Fake smile? Please! You look too real. If you're faking, then you deserve an Oscar!"

Aarav (winking):
"Send my name to Bollywood. Maybe I'll finally have a backup career."

(Everyone laughs again. Aarav stirs his cold coffee, staring into it a moment too long before snapping back into character.)

“Come on, guys, now back to classroom, Professor Sinha will take very interesting class today,” Kabir said.

Aarav, with friends, attended the lecture but his thoughts were roaming somewhere else. After the lecture, everyone moved out except Aarav. There is momentary silence. Aarav wanders into a deserted classroom. Sunlight filters through dusty windows. He sits at the last bench.

Aarav's thoughts:
"They think I'm the chilled one, the unshakable one. If only they knew how much energy it takes to keep smiling. My laughter is louder than my screams inside... because if they heard those screams, they'd run."

(He takes out his mobile phone. Dozens of unread messages. He scrolls, pretends to type, then switches off the screen and keeps it face-down.)

Aarav (whispering):
"No one notices. Maybe I've become too good at hiding. So, one thing is very certain that I am a good actor." With clumsy smile, he starts his bike and runs to home.

Everything is well settled at home. He took off his shoes, put them on the rack, and sank into the sofa and stared watching TV.

"Dinner's ready!" his mother called from the kitchen.

Aarav walked in with a grin plastered on. "Smells amazing, Mom." He filled his plate, cracked a joke about his father's obsession with the news, and laughed when everyone else did. But when he returned to his room, closing the door behind him, the mask fell off. The smile crumbled, his shoulders sank, and he sat on the floor, drained. The lights are dim. Books scattered on the bed.

Aarav's inner conflict:
"All day I wear the mask. Strong Aarav. Funny Aarav. Confident Aarav. But here... there's no one to fool."

(He stares at the mirror. His reflection looks back with a tired, hollow face. He forces a smile. The reflection smiles too, mockingly.)

Aarav (angrily at the mirror):
"Stop pretending! Who are you fooling? They don't care. They never will."

(He grips the table, trembling. His breath quickens. A tear slips down his cheek. He wipes it roughly.)

"I wear the mask because it's easier. Because the world loves smiles, not scars. But sometimes, I wonder—what if one person could see through it? What if someone cared enough to stay when the mask falls? Would I still need to hide?"

(A faint smile crosses his lips, bittersweet. He pulls the blanket over his face, whispering to himself.)

Aarav:
"Maybe tomorrow, I'll wear the mask again. Maybe tomorrow, they'll laugh with me. And maybe... someday... someone will see the real me."

Aarav (softly, breaking):
"I'm so tired... tired of fake smiling... tired of holding it all in."

(He falls to the floor, hugging his knees, muffling sobs into his arms. His body shakes as he lets out what he has hidden all day. A long silence follows. Just the sound of a broken boy trying not to be heard.)

He opened his diary and wrote:
"Today, I wore the mask. Nobody saw through it. Maybe nobody ever will."

And then, in smaller letters:
"27 days left."

The ceiling fan whirred above, indifferent. Outside, the world laughed and carried on. Inside, Aarav quietly wondered: "Am I already invisible?"

"What feels permanent today may be tomorrow's distant memory."

Day 4 – Flashbacks of Laughter

"Pain is real, but so is the possibility of change."

It was Saturday afternoon. Aarav lay sprawled on his bed, staring at the ceiling fan spinning in lazy circles. He hadn't opened his books, hadn't touched his phone, hadn't spoken much all day.

The silence pressed down, until—like a cruel trick—his mind wandered into old reels of laughter.

That Rainy Day---

He saw himself at ten years old, splashing barefoot in puddles after a heavy monsoon. His mother had shouted from the balcony, "Aarav, you'll catch a fever!" But his father had only chuckled, saying, "Let him be, he's alive today."

He remembered the rush of cold rain, the squeal of joy when a friend joined him, the feeling of being infinite for just those few minutes.

"When did I forget how to feel alive like that?" he whispered, a lump in his throat.

That Birthday---

Another memory surfaced. His 14th birthday. Friends crowded his small living room, cake smeared on his face, balloons bouncing against the ceiling. He had laughed so hard that his stomach hurt.

Rahul had hugged him then, shouting, "Don't you ever dare stop smiling, idiot!"

Now Aarav touched his own lips, almost surprised to feel how foreign a real smile had become.

Aarav muffled: "You see, you did laugh once. You weren't always like this."

"But what's the use? Those days are gone. People have changed. I've changed."

"Or maybe the laughter is still there... you just buried it."

"Buried so deep I'll never find it again."

Suddenly, the day of his result flashed in his mind when his father's encouragement had helped him lot.

That day, Aarav was sitting with his father at the table after a failed math test. Aarav had been on the verge of tears, but his father had ruffled his hair and said,

"Marks aren't everything, my son. One failure doesn't mean you're a failure."

The warmth of that moment hit him like a wave. His father rarely showed affection, but that day he had. Aarav closed his eyes now, whispering: "Why don't those words work anymore, Papa?"

In the evening the laughter of neighbors floated through the window—children playing cricket, mothers gossiping, someone's radio blasting an old filmy song. The world sounded alive, but in Aarav's chest, everything felt hollow.

He scribbled in his diary:
"Memories of laughter feel heavier than silence. They remind me of what I've lost, not what I had."

Then, after a pause, he added:
"26 days left."

Before bed, Aarav stood at the mirror. He forced a laugh—loud, awkward, fake. The sound echoed off the walls until it cracked into a sob.

He sank to the floor, clutching his chest. "I wonder... will anyone ever remember me laughing?"

"Even broken wings can learn to fly again."

Day 5 – Hidden Tears

"You are not weak for feeling; you are human for surviving."

The morning sun spilled through the curtains, but it felt harsh, unwanted. Aarav sat at the edge of his bed, his diary open before him. The pages already carried the weight of four days, and today would be no different.

"I wonder if this diary will cry when I'm gone," he thought bitterly.

At college, the classes blurred past him. He laughed when others laughed, nodded when asked questions, but his mind wasn't there. When the bell rang, everyone rushed to the canteen. Aarav slipped quietly into the library instead.

Sitting at the far corner, hidden behind tall shelves, he pressed his face into his sleeve. That's when it happened—the tears came, hot and sudden.

"Why here? Why now?" he panicked, looking around. Luckily, no one noticed. The silence of the library guarded his secret.

"See? You're weak. Can't even hold it in anymore."

“No. I’m strong. No one saw. No one ever sees.”

“But don’t you want someone to see? Someone to ask?”

“...I don’t know.”

He wiped his face quickly, inhaling sharply. When footsteps approached, he buried his head in a book he hadn’t even opened.

He remembered being thirteen, crying after failing a science project. His parents had been arguing in the next room. Not wanting to add to their burden, he had stuffed a pillow into his mouth to muffle his sobs.

"Since then, I’ve always cried in silence," he thought. “And no one ever knew.”

His mother peeked into his room in the evening. “Everything okay, Aarav?”

“Yeah, Mamma,” he smiled, tapping at his phone screen though it was blank. “Just tired.”

She nodded, satisfied, and left.

The moment the door closed, Aarav buried his face in his pillow. This time, he let the tears flow until his chest hurt.

"How do tears always find me when no one else does?"

That night, he wrote in diary with shaky letters:
“I don’t cry in front of people anymore. Maybe I’m afraid they’ll see the real me.”

Below it, he added:
“25 days left.”

As he turned off the light, his pillow was still damp. The room was silent, but he whispered into the darkness:

I smile...
but the smile is stitched with trembling threads.
I laugh...
but the echo carries cracks no one hears.
I walk in sunlight,
yet the shadows cling tighter to my skin.

These eyes,
they hold oceans—
oceans I never let spill,
for fear the world would drown in truths
it does not want to see.

Hidden tears...
they are the heaviest kind.
They do not fall,
they do not cleanse,
they burn...
etching scars on the inside of the soul,
where no hand can reach,
no balm can soothe.

I wear my strength like armor,
polished, unbreakable—
but beneath, I am glass,
shattered into silent fragments.
Still, I hide.
Because the world kneels before courage,
not weakness.
It praises the strong back,
not the trembling heart.

And so—
my tears remain secrets,
salted prayers whispered to the night.
Unseen.
Unheard.
Unfelt.

But if ever...
someone were to look deeper,
past the smile, past the laughter,
past the mask I have learned too well...
they would find a river aching for release,
a soul waiting to be held,
a silence begging to be understood.

Until then—
I will drown quietly,
behind eyes that sparkle,
and a smile that lies.

"Maybe my tears are the only ones who know me anymore."

"Every tear shed waters the seed of resilience."

Day 6 – The Diary Begins

"The mind replays pain, but it can also be taught to replay hope."

The morning felt heavy. Aarav stared at his reflection in the mirror, dark circles under his eyes, lips pressed thin. He ran his hand through his hair and muttered, "At least you're still here, huh?"

The mirror didn't answer. But the diary on his desk almost seemed to be waiting. Aarav finds a silent companion in his diary, a turning point that starts giving shape to his inner voice.

He opened to a fresh page and wrote:
"Hello, Diary. You're the only one who'll listen. I don't know if I'll make it through these 30 days, but at least you'll know me better than anyone else ever did."

He paused, staring at the ink, then scribbled below:
"Can a diary be a friend? Or is that just me going crazy?"

At college, all day, Aarav kept thinking of the diary. During class, while others scrolled through their phones, he scribbled notes in its margins:

"I smiled today, but it was fake."

"Why does laughter sound like noise now?"

"Does anyone else feel invisible?"

Each sentence lightened him, just a little. In the afternoon, a memory returned. Rahul—his old best friend. Back in middle school, Aarav had poured his heart out to him once, about how lonely he felt at home. Rahul had promised, "I'll always be there."

But time had pulled them apart. New schools, new circles, new priorities. Aarav now wrote in the diary:
"I guess you're Rahul now. At least you can't leave me."

Back in his room in evening, Aarav placed the diary on his lap and began writing like he was speaking aloud:

"Dear Diary, today I realized something. People are busy, people are blind, but you're here. You don't judge. You don't interrupt. Maybe I should have started talking to you years ago."

For the first time in weeks, he felt a strange calmness. His chest loosened, as though the pages had absorbed his burden.

"See? You found someone to listen."

"But it's just paper."

"Sometimes paper is kinder than people."

He smiled faintly at that thought, though it didn't last long. But he felt that the diary responds as if it "talks back" like a friend.

Aarav: (writing) Why does everything feel so heavy today? I'm smiling outside but inside I'm breaking. I don't even know what's real anymore.

Diary: (as if the pages whisper back)
Tell me, Aarav. Don't hold back. I'm here. What's making you feel this way?

Aarav:
It's like I'm trapped between two lives. The one everyone expects from me and the one I actually want to live. If I keep pleasing them, I lose myself. If I choose me, I lose them. How do I decide, How?

Diary:
Sometimes, you don't have to decide right away. Sometimes you just need to let yourself feel. It's okay to be confused. It's okay to be tired. You're not weak for feeling lost.

Aarav:
But everyone thinks I'm strong. They think I have it together. I don't want to disappoint them. I'm so tired of pretending.

Diary:
Strength isn't about pretending, Aarav. It's about being honest, even if it's just here, with me. You're already strong because you're facing your feelings instead of running from them.

Aarav:
I wish I had someone like you in real life. Someone who listens without judging or interrupting.

Diary:
I may just be paper and ink, but I'm your safe place. Still, don't forget there are people out there who can listen too – maybe not perfectly, but they can try. You're not as alone as you feel.

Aarav:
It's strange, isn't it? Talking to a diary and feeling like it's a friend.

Diary:
Not strange at all. Sometimes the quietest spaces are where you hear yourself the loudest.

Aarav:
Do you think I'll ever find peace?

Diary:
I think you're already walking toward it, one word at a time. Every time you write, you let some pain out. Keep going. You're healing, even if you don't see it yet.

Aarav:
Thank you... for being here when nobody else is.

Diary:
Always, Aarav. I'm here as long as you need me. Keep writing.

Finally at 12 p.m. night, he signed off:
"I'll keep writing until the end. 24 days left."
Before switching off the light, Aarav placed the diary beside his pillow. For the first time, he whispered not into the darkness, but to the book:

"Goodnight, friend."

"One kinder thought toward yourself today is a victory."

Day 7 – Masks We Wear

"Loneliness whispers lies; connection speaks truth."

The alarm buzzed at 6:30 a.m. Aarav groaned, buried under his blanket. He wanted to disappear into the mattress. But then a thought jolted him awake: "If I look miserable, they'll ask questions. I can't handle questions." So he dragged himself to the mirror. With practiced precision, he fixed his hair, splashed water on his face, and stretched his lips into a smile. It felt stiff, but it would do.

"There. Mask on."

"Bro, where were you yesterday? We missed you at practice!" a classmate called in college.

"Oh, had some work... you know, family stuff," Aarav replied with a grin. His voice was smooth, casual, convincing.

They laughed together, and nobody noticed how his hands clenched under the desk.

He slipped away between classes, locking himself in a bathroom stall. Leaning against the cold wall, he whispered:

"You're good at this. Nobody suspects a thing."

"But isn't that the problem? They only see the mask."

"If they saw the real you, they'd run. This way, you're safe. What a painful skill of faking normalcy while suffocating inside."

He splashed water on his face, wiping away the faint redness around his eyes. The mask was back in place.

A memory stirred—his English teacher once telling his parents, "Aarav is such a cheerful boy! Always smiling, always polite."

His parents had beamed with pride that day. Aarav had smiled too, but inside, he'd thought: "If only they knew."

Aarav moved through the crowded streets, blending in with the flow of people, yet feeling entirely alone. The hum of conversations, the laughter spilling from cafés, the distant honking of traffic—all of it pressed against him like a constant reminder that he was performing. He smiled at a passing acquaintance, nodded at a casual greeting, laughed at a joke he didn't find funny. Each act was precise, polished, careful. On the surface, he looked at ease, almost ordinary. Inside, he seethed.

He hated it. Every small gesture of pretense felt like a betrayal of himself. He hated that he had to measure his reactions, edit his words, hide his true feelings. It was exhausting, suffocating. And yet, paradoxically, a part of him admired it. The mask—though heavy—was a shield. It allowed him to navigate the scrutiny of others, to remain untouched by judgment or rejection. In his own quiet, conflicted way, he praised himself for being clever enough to survive without exposing the raw, vulnerable parts of who he really was.

Even in moments of solitude, the tension lingered. Sitting at a park bench, watching children play without a care, Aarav envied their freedom. Their laughter was genuine, unfiltered. They didn't wear masks to shield themselves from the world; they were simply themselves. He wished he could do the same, yet he knew he couldn't. Not yet.

At home, he peeled off his outer layers of civility, the careful posture, the practiced smiles, and stared into the mirror. He studied his reflection, searching for the real Aarav behind the eyes. Was he the confident actor the world saw, or the anxious, cautious boy he kept hidden? He didn't know. And that uncertainty gnawed at him more than any social interaction ever could.

Even the small objects around him seemed to mirror his inner conflict. The worn-out notebook on his desk, filled with sketches and fragments of poetry he had never shown anyone, reminded him of the parts of himself he had locked away. The clock on the wall ticked on, indifferent to his struggle, marking each passing moment in which he played a role instead of living authentically.

He longed for freedom—the courage to speak without hesitation, to let his silence be his own, to be raw and unguarded. But even as he imagined tearing the mask away, fear tightened around him. What if, once exposed, he wasn't enough? What if the world recoiled at the unpolished truth?

So, day after day, Aarav walked a fine line. He hated the mask he wore, yet he clung to it like a lifeline. He scolded himself for hiding, but he also admired his ability to navigate life safely. In this delicate balance between self-reproach and self-preservation, between vulnerability and survival, Aarav existed—a boy caught between who he was and who the world demanded him to be.

At dinner, his mother chatted about groceries, his father about work. Aarav chimed in with small jokes, even making them laugh.

But later in his room, the diary received the truth:

"I've become an actor in my own life. Smiles for the world, tears for my pillow. I wonder if anyone would recognize me without the mask."

As night settled over the city, Aarav sat by his window, watching the lights flicker in the distance. The mask rested beside him, heavy but familiar, and he wondered if he would ever have the courage to set it aside completely. Somewhere deep inside, a quiet voice whispered that the real Aarav still existed, waiting for a moment of bravery to surface. And until that day came, he would continue this delicate dance—half hidden, half revealed—torn between who he was and who he had learned to be.

He signed off:
"23 days left. Today, my mask saved me. Or maybe it killed me a little more."

Before sleeping, Aarav stared outside the window and whispered:
"Maybe if I keep pretending long enough... I'll forget who I really am."

The mask, invisible yet heavy, stayed on even in the dark.

"Reaching out is not a sign of weakness—it is proof of life."

Day 8 – The Silent Screams

Courage doesn't always roar; sometimes it's just a quiet decision to stay."

Aarav woke to the piercing sound of his alarm at 6:45 a.m. His head throbbed from another night of almost no sleep. Every muscle ached, but worse was the weight pressing on his chest—an invisible hand squeezing, refusing to let go.

"I feel like I'm screaming... but no one can hear it," he muttered, staring at the ceiling.

"Why does it hurt so much to be alive?"

"Because you're trying to feel something... anything. And it all hurts."

"Then scream. Make it loud."

"No one would hear. No one cares. Better to stay quiet."

The pain wasn't physical. It wasn't something that could be bandaged or healed with medicine. It was inside—quiet, persistent, invisible.

Aarav walked through the hallways in college, ears ringing with laughter, chatter, and footsteps. Each sound felt amplified—like a cruel reminder that he was drowning in silence while the world carried on.

During break, he leaned against a wall and exhaled sharply. Nobody noticed. Nobody ever noticed.

"Maybe that's the point," he thought. "I'm invisible. I've always been invisible."

He remembered being fourteen, alone in the playground after a fight with his father. He had yelled, cursed, stomped—then realized the tears streaming down his face made him sound weak. From that day, he decided: If you scream, do it silently. Inside.

It had worked for years. The silent screams had become a habit, a shadow that followed him everywhere.

The years passed, but the wounds didn't heal. They just... collected dust, buried under routine, school, grades, and the heavy expectation of others. My laughter became mechanical. My smiles, forced.

I often wondered if anyone could see past the mask. If anyone could recognize the storm raging inside me.

No one notices.

His mother knocked softly on the door. "Aarav, dinner is ready."

"Coming, Mom," he said, voice flat. He put on the mask once more, forcing a laugh when his father joked about the news.

Then, alone in his room, he curled on the floor, letting the silent screams erupt through tears, fists, and trembling limbs. The diary lay open beside him, empty but waiting.

He wrote his diary in jagged letters:
"Silent screams hurt more than words ever could. Maybe because they echo forever inside."

Below, he noted:
"22 days left."

As he lay down, the night pressing against his window, Aarav whispered:
"Maybe the world is deaf. But the screams... they're mine. They're all mine."

And in that silence, he felt the strange mix of despair and a tiny pulse of recognition—he was still alive.

Aarav's inner turmoil reaches a peak, with the contrast between his outer quiet and inner chaos.

"Tonight you stayed. That is enough."

Day 9 – Stranger's Smile

"Our scars are not the end of our story; they are the chapters of survival."

The morning air was crisp, the sky streaked with pale gold. Aarav walked to college, his backpack heavy, his shoulders stooped. The world felt distant, muffled, as if he were moving through a dream that he didn't want to wake from.

"Another day. Another mask," he thought.

At the bus stop, he noticed a small girl struggling with her balloon, the string tangled around her fingers. Before he could think, he bent down and untangled it.

"Thank you, mister!" she said, her eyes bright and wide.

Aarav nodded, offering a faint smile. She beamed at him, then skipped away.

Something about her smile—pure, unpretentious, innocent—stayed with him. He couldn't explain why, but it scratched at the tight armor around his heart.

“It’s just a kid. Nothing happened. Move on.”

“But... why do I feel... light? Like something inside me woke up?”

“Don’t let it fool you. Life hasn’t changed. This is meaningless.”

“Or maybe... not everything is meaningless.”

He remembered a forgotten kindness of his senior when he was in middle school, having lost his cricket match, sitting alone on the bench. The senior boy had come over, handed him a chocolate, and said: “You played well. Don’t be sad.”

He hadn’t remembered that day in years, but now the memory made him catch his breath.

"Maybe kindness... matters," he whispered.

During lectures, he couldn’t stop thinking about the girl’s smile. It was irrational, fleeting, but it lingered like a faint melody. For the first time in days, his chest didn’t feel like it was being crushed by invisible hands.

Even in the bustling corridors, he felt a tiny thread of connection to the world, delicate but undeniable. On returning home, Aarav goes to the park which had always been his silent refuge, a place where he could sit alone and let the world drift by without noticing him.

Aarav was lost in his thoughts when a voice broke through the gray silence.

“Hey... are you okay?”

He froze. His instinct was to ignore, to vanish into the shadows of the park, but he glanced up. A man, maybe in his late forties, with kind eyes and a gentle smile, stood a few feet away. He didn't seem judgmental, only curious.

"I... I'm fine," Aarav mumbled, more out of reflex than truth.

He didn't move closer, didn't push. Just observed quietly. Then he asked the question that would linger in Aarav's mind long after he left:

"Why are you still here?"

Aarav heard his internal chaos silently.

"The words hit me harder than I expected. Why am I still here? The question wasn't loud. It wasn't accusing. But it was a mirror, reflecting all the doubts, all the despair I had buried so deep."

"I don't know, I thought. I really don't know."

"I wanted to run. I wanted to disappear into the mist and let the world erase me. But something in his calm gaze stopped me."

Suddenly he shouts-

"You... you don't understand," he said finally, his voice breaking. "No one notices me. I'm... I'm just... here."

Stanger nodded, calmly. "I think I understand more than you realize. But being here matters, doesn't it? If you weren't, you wouldn't be walking through this park right now."

Aarav wanted to scream at him, to push him away. But he stayed silent. There was something in his voice—steady, unshakable—that he hadn't heard in a long time. Someone treating him like he mattered.

The stranger crouched slightly, so he was closer to my eye level, and asked gently:

"If life feels unbearable, and you feel like giving up... why not give it a chance to surprise you instead?"

Surprise me? Aarav thought. What could life possibly have to offer?

"I... I don't know," he admitted. "Maybe... maybe nothing."

The stranger smiled softly. "Maybe everything. But you won't know until you try. And trying doesn't mean you have to do everything at once. Just... take one step. One small step."

Aarav walked home slowly, the words echoing in his head: Just take one small step.

It didn't solve anything. It didn't erase the darkness that had been my constant companion. But it planted a seed—tiny, fragile, almost laughable in its weakness.

He muttered-
"One step... I can try that. Maybe I don't have to figure everything out today. Maybe I can just... be here, one moment at a time."

"For the first time in weeks, I didn't feel completely invisible. Someone had noticed me. Someone had asked the question I had been too afraid to ask myself."

"And that is enough... for now."

At home, Aarav wrote in his diary for the first time that day with a small, hesitant hope:

"A girl's smile today... it was nothing, and yet it felt like everything. Maybe... maybe there's a world worth noticing after all."

"I didn't know, but that moment—the stranger's question, his quiet presence—was the first spark. It was the beginning of a journey I wasn't sure I was ready for, but my life had chosen for me anyway."

"Maybe... maybe being here still matters."

He drew a tiny smiley face next to the words—a childish act, but somehow comforting.

Below it, he added:
"21 days left."

Before sleeping, he whispered into the darkness, as if testing the feeling:
"Could life... be more than pain? Just maybe?"

And for the first time in days, the thought didn't scare him.

"You are stronger for every hurt you've endured."

Day 10 – A Ray of Light

"Single step forward is greater than a thousand regrets behind."

The sun spilled gold across the city streets. Aarav walked to college, backpack slung carelessly over one shoulder. His body moved, but his mind lingered on the shadows of yesterday.

"Stranger's smile... nice enough, but it won't change anything," he muttered under his breath.

In the college courtyard, Aarav noticed a group of students struggling to set up a charity stall. Tables wobbled, banners flapped in the wind, and volunteers seemed frazzled. Without thinking, he stepped forward.

"Here, let me help," he offered quietly.

They looked at him, surprised, but gratefully handed him a stack of flyers.

As he arranged the tables and straightened the banners, something inside him stirred. He watched people smile, take flyers, nod in thanks. The world seemed... alive.

“Don’t get carried away. It’s just helping with a stall. Nothing important.” He uttered.

“Maybe. But... I felt useful. And it wasn’t painful.”

“It’s temporary. Wait until tomorrow.”

“Or maybe... this is what a small spark feels like.”
Aarav remembered helping a neighbor’s child learn to ride a bicycle. The joy in the kid’s eyes had made him feel... powerful, in a small way. He hadn’t thought of that in years, but now the memory returned vividly.

"I forgot I could feel useful... even in small ways," he whispered.

The ring of the mobile phone put the brakes on his thoughts for a while. He took it out of his jeans and saw, it was Meera calling. He picked up the call and said-

“Hi Meera! Hope all well? Anything major”

“Nothing dear. All well. Just remembering you.”

“Actually I am in mid of one of my painting. Just wish to show you.”

“Are you free? Please come for 10 minutes”

Aarav replied- “Ok..Ok...don’t say please buddy...I am coming.”

He reached the place within ten minutes. But as he passed by the small art studio at the far corner of the community center, a faint glimmer of color caught his eye. The door stood slightly ajar, and inside, Meera was painting. She always seemed to lose herself in her strokes, as if the brush carried her heartbeat.

Something urged him to pause. Maybe it was hesitation. Maybe it was the quiet pull of her presence. For reasons he couldn't explain, Aarav stepped in.

Meera (noticing him, her face lighting up):
"Aarav! You came. I wasn't sure you would... but I hoped."

Aarav (shrugging, his tone flat but not unkind):
"I almost didn't. Didn't feel like talking to anyone. But... I guess I didn't want to be alone either."

Meera (softly, putting her brush down):
"Sometimes we just need to sit with someone. No words required. Just presence."

Aarav lowered himself into a chair. The studio smelled of paint—sharp yet oddly comforting. The walls were covered in canvases: storms of color, fields of light, and faces captured mid-emotion.

On the easel in front of her stood a half-finished painting. Aarav's eyes lingered on it: dark grays dominating the edges, with a single burst of yellow and white piercing through the middle. It reminded him of dawn trying to break through a restless night.

Aarav (pointing slightly):
"What's this one supposed to be?"

Meera (tilting her head, smiling faintly):
"What do you see in it? I need to know, and this is the reason for what you are here."

Aarav (hesitant, almost defensive):
"I'm not good at this art stuff. I wouldn't know."

Meera (gently, leaning closer):

"There's no right or wrong in seeing, Aarav. Just... feel it. What does it say to you?"

For a long moment, he stared at the canvas. His eyes followed the rays of yellow stretching outward, pushing against the dark. Slowly, almost unwillingly, his voice softened.

Aarav:
"It looks like... light fighting its way through. Like... no matter how strong the darkness is, the light doesn't give up."

Meera's smile widened, not in triumph but in understanding.

"That's exactly what I hoped someone would see. You know, Aarav... people think light removes darkness. But it doesn't. It coexists. The sun rises every day, but the night always comes back. The meaning lies not in erasing the dark... but in choosing to notice the light when it arrives."

Aarav swallowed hard. Her words struck something in him, something that had been buried under weeks of hopelessness.

Aarav (voice low):
"Do you really believe life can be meaningful? Even when it feels so... empty?"

Meera (turning to him, her eyes steady and kind):
"Yes. Because meaning isn't something waiting outside for us to find. It's something we create. Sometimes through pain, sometimes through gratitude. Look at this painting—if the darkness wasn't there, the light wouldn't look so beautiful."

Aarav stared again at the canvas. His chest tightened, but this time it wasn't with despair—it was with the faintest flicker of recognition. He had been so focused on the shadows of his life that he hadn't noticed the possibility of brightness.

Aarav (whispering):
"You painted this for me, didn't you?"

Meera (after a pause, her smile softening):
"I painted it for hope. But yes... I wanted you to see it. Because sometimes when words can't reach someone, colors still can."

Silence stretched between them, but it wasn't awkward. The kind of silence where hearts quietly speak without noise. Aarav leaned forward, his hand brushing the wooden frame of the painting as though trying to absorb its warmth.

Aarav (voice trembling):
"It feels like it's telling me... I'm not finished. That even if everything looks broken, maybe tomorrow can still be different."

Meera (placing her hand gently over his):
"That's the truth, Aarav. Your story isn't over. And even if it feels dark now, the fact that you're here, breathing, seeing, feeling—that itself means the light hasn't left you. You just need to face it."

For the first time in weeks, Aarav's lips curved into a small, hesitant, but genuine smile. His eyes grew moist, but they were not tears of helplessness—they were tears of relief, of something rediscovered.

Aarav (with a shaky laugh):
"Maybe... maybe I should stop counting shadows and start looking for these rays instead."

Meera (warmly):
"And when you do, you'll realize they've always been there. Waiting for you to notice."

One thing more dear, she added:

"Life will always have its shadows, but it will also always offer us light. What we choose to focus on shapes our experience of living. Gratitude for even the smallest ray of hope can transform despair into strength."

The golden light from the setting sun filtered through the window, spilling across Aarav's face. He felt it on his skin—warm, alive, and real. For the first time in a long while, he wasn't just existing. He was beginning to feel.

Back in his room, he opened his diary. The page felt heavy with the weight of ten days, but he wrote with a careful optimism:

"Today, I helped. Not for anyone else. Not for praise. I helped, and it felt... like something inside me woke up."

He added a drawing of a small sun rising over a horizon, clumsy but meaningful.

Below it, he noted:
"20 days left."

Lying on his bed, Aarav stared at the ceiling. The shadows didn't feel as thick. The night didn't feel as heavy.
"Maybe... there's a reason to see tomorrow," he whispered, almost scared to admit it.
And for the first time in ten days, he let himself linger on the thought—just for a moment—without fear.

"You walked today. Tomorrow, you will walk again."

Day 11 – Anger Within

"Healing is not about erasing the past; it is about rewriting its meaning."

Aarav woke up with a tension coiled tightly in his heart, heavier than usual. The morning sunlight poured through the blinds, but it did nothing to lift the dark cloud inside him.

"Why is everything so... unfair?" he muttered, pacing his room.

The world felt unjust, and for the first time in days, the anger bubbled to the surface—raw, hot, impossible to ignore.

In class, a group of students laughed at a minor mistake one of their classmates made. Aarav's face tightened. "It's not funny. How can you laugh at someone else's pain?"

He remembered a time in middle school when a bully had taken his notebook and tore it in front of everyone. He had wanted to hit the boy, scream, throw things. But he had swallowed it all, tears and fury mixed together.

"I've always swallowed everything... until now," he thought.

He clenched his fists, trying to control the storm inside. His heart pounded, rage threatening to spill over.

"This world is cruel... people are careless... life doesn't care," he whispered.

"Why are you angry? It's just the world. You can't fix it."

"Maybe not. But I feel it. Every injustice, every fake smile, every cruelty—it hurts me."

"Anger won't save you. It won't bring relief."

"Or maybe it's the only thing keeping me awake... keeping me human."

Thud...thud...thud...heavy solid sound from the door. Aarav opened the door and saw Meera and Rahul were smiling there. Rahul spanked his back lightly: "Hi, boss! What's up? Looking shaky..! Is everything ok?"
He stepped in the room and played music of Kenny G.

Aarav is pacing around, running his hands through his hair, muttering to himself. His notebook lies open on the table with half-written lines, scribbles, and scratched-out words. He suddenly throws the pen across the room.

Aarav (snapping): "Damn it! I can't even decide what the hell I want. One second I think yes, the next second no. I feel like my brain's stuck in traffic and all the signals are red!"

He collapses on the bed, face buried in the pillow. Meera and Rahul, who had been sitting on the floor with chips and cola, exchange looks.

Meera (with mock seriousness): "Breaking news: Local boy loses war against traffic lights inside his head. Ambulance stuck too. More updates at 9."

Rahul (snorts, spraying cola from his mouth): "Pfff—stop, Meera! Now my nose is burning. Aarav, see what you're doing, you're killing me here!"

Aarav lifts his head slightly, still frowning but lips twitch a bit.

Aarav: "You guys are ridiculous. I'm serious, buddy... this indecision thing is eating me alive. I feel... useless."

Meera crawls onto the bed and flops beside him dramatically.

Meera: "Useless? Bro, I saw you decide between two flavors of chips in two seconds flat last week. That's not useless-that's world record speed."

Rahul (joining in): "Exactly. And don't forget, you also decided to ditch my playlist for your sad boy songs. Very bold move, very hurtful, but still—decision taken."

Aarav groans, hiding his face again, but now they can hear the muffled sound of his laugh.

Aarav (voice muffled): "That's not the same thing... these are serious choices. My future's at stake. What if I screw it up?"

Meera (rolling onto her stomach, poking him in the shoulder): "What if? Bro, life's not a bomb you're diffusing. It's not like: cut the red wire and boom, everything's gone. You can still tape the wires back together."

Rahul (grabbing the thrown pen from the floor, twirling it like a sword): "And worst case? You screw up. So what? We'll laugh at you, call you names, then still show up with pizza. That's our job description as friends."

Aarav finally sits up, rubbing his temples but smiling faintly.

Aarav: "You guys really think laughing at me will fix things?"

Meera (grinning): "Of course. That's our therapy method—cheap, effective, side effect: occasional hiccups, ha ha ha."

Rahul: "Plus, who said you're supposed to have all answers right now? Even Google takes time to load sometimes, and it's literally God with Wi-Fi."

Aarav chuckles and shakes his head. His body visibly relaxes as the tension softens.

Aarav (smirking): "Fine. You two clowns win. I'll... try not to punch myself for being confused."

Meera (raising her cola can): "Good boy! That's step one. Step two: you buy us ice cream when your brain stops being a drama queen."

Rahul (clinking his can with hers): "And if it doesn't stop, we'll still take the ice cream. Win-win."

Aarav finally laughs openly, shaking his head at their antics. His frustration isn't gone, but it feels lighter, manageable—with Meera and Rahul sitting there like anchors keeping him steady.

Later that night...

The room is quieter now. Meera and Rahul have gone, leaving behind empty cola cans and chip crumbs like battle scars of their "therapy session." Aarav lies on his bed, staring at the ceiling fan slowly rotating.

Aarav (thinking):
"God... I was about to explode today. My head felt like it was tearing itself apart. I hate this feeling—this helplessness. Like I'm standing at a crossroads with no map, no signboard, and every direction looks wrong. It scares me."

He exhales deeply, running a hand across his face. Then, almost involuntarily, a smile creeps onto his lips as he recalls Meera's mock-news voice and Rahul choking on cola.

Aarav (thinking, softer):
"But then those idiots showed up. Instead of dumping heavy advice on me, they just... made me laugh. Mocked my overthinking, turned my storm into a comedy show. And weirdly... it worked. I still don't have the answers, but I don't feel like dying under the weight of questions anymore."

Lying on the floor, Aarav whispered to himself:
"Anger... maybe you're not my enemy. Maybe you're my signal to wake up. To notice. To fight... even if I don't know what I'm fighting for yet."

The room was still, but for the first time in a long while, Aarav felt a pulse—small, fierce, undeniable.
He wrote furiously in his diary:
"Anger is still alive inside me. I can't ignore it. Maybe I shouldn't. Maybe it's proof that I still care... that I still feel. And maybe that's a reason to keep going."

Below it, he scribbled:
"19 days left."

The ceiling fan hums, steady and calm. Aarav pulls the pillow closer under his head.

Aarav (thinking, final):
"Maybe I don't need to figure everything out tonight. Maybe having these two clowns around is enough to keep me from drowning in my own head. I guess... even if I'm stuck at a red light inside, at least I'm not waiting there alone."

He closes his eyes, the hint of a smile still on his face, as sleep slowly pulls him into a quieter place.

"Your story is still unfolding—don't close the book yet."

Day 12 – The Teacher's Words

"Comparison steals joy; self-acceptance restores it."

The morning sun poured into the classroom, but Aarav barely noticed. The tick of the wall clock seemed louder than usual. Students bent over their notebooks, copying the algorithm that Ms. Jemima had written neatly on the board. Pens scratched, papers rustled—but one desk in the middle row seemed frozen in time.

Aarav sat there, his head tilted slightly, his eyes dull, staring at the blank page before him. His pen rested loosely between his fingers, as if he had forgotten why he even picked it up. His once sharp answers, his cheerful voice, his curious spark—all had dimmed in recent weeks. Thoughts of yesterday's anger still lingered, heavy and insistent.

"Nothing changes. Life just keeps throwing pain at you," he muttered.

Ms. Jemima, a teacher not just by profession but by heart, noticed it immediately. For days she had observed the gloom on Aarav's face, the silence in his eyes. She knew the difference between a lazy student and a wounded one—and Aarav, she sensed, was wounded inside. She paused mid-lecture. She walked toward Aarav, smiling gently.

"Aarav, you've been unusually quiet lately. Is everything okay?"

Aarav's heart skipped a beat. Nobody had asked him that in weeks. The mask of indifference threatened to crumble.

"Why does she care?" he thought.

He managed a faint nod. "Yes... I'm fine, ma'am."

She turned to the class, her chalk still in hand, and then paused. She looked at Aarav for a fleeting moment, then quickly shifted her gaze to the entire room. She did not want to single him out.

"Children," she said, setting the chalk down, "close your notebooks for a while. Today, before we continue, I want to talk to you about something far more important than history."

A few groans of protest came from the back benches, but most students looked up, surprised. Aarav did not move, but the change in her tone made his ears listen.

"Life," she began softly, "is a bigger classroom than this one. It gives us lessons every day—but not always with textbooks."

Some students exchanged curious glances. Aarav's fingers tightened faintly around his pen.

"You know," she continued, "I once had a piece of chalk that broke while I was writing on the board." She lifted a fresh chalk from the tray, held it up, and snapped it into two with a deliberate crack. The class gasped lightly.

"Now," she smiled gently, holding the broken halves, "is this chalk useless now?"

"No, ma'am," said Meera from the first row.

"It can still write, ma'am!" another boy chimed in.

"Exactly." Ms. Jemima nodded. "Even broken, it can still write, still teach, still leave its mark. Children, people are just like this. Sometimes life breaks us with pain, with failures, with things we don't understand. But does that mean we are useless?"

The class was silent now. The words seemed to hang in the air. Aarav's eyes, for the first time, lifted briefly towards her, then fell again.

She noticed, but did not let her gaze linger. Instead, she began walking slowly between the desks.

"Once upon a time," she said, her voice warm and steady, "there was a little boy I knew. Very smart, very cheerful. But one day... life gave him a test much harder than any exam. He felt alone. He stopped smiling. He thought—'What's the use of trying? Everything is meaningless.'"

A murmur ran through the class. The story had caught their attention. Aarav's ears perked up.

"But then," Ms. Jemima continued, "one day, the boy saw a bird with one weak wing. Everyone thought it would never fly again. But do you know what it did?"

"What, ma'am?" asked Rahul eagerly.

"It tried," she said simply. "Again and again, the bird tried to spread its wings. And one day—it lifted itself into the sky. Not as smoothly as before, not as strong as others, but it flew. And in that moment, the boy realized something: if a bird with a broken wing can still fly, then a person with a broken heart can still live, still rise."

A hush fell over the room.

Aarav's chest tightened. His pen rolled off the desk with a soft thud, but he didn't notice. His eyes were fixed on the floor, his mind replaying the words. Ms. Jemima bent to pick up the pen and gently placed it back on his desk without a word. Then she straightened and addressed the class again.

"Children, do you know what happens when dark clouds cover the sky?" she asked.

"It rains?" a boy guessed.

"Yes," she smiled. "And after rain?"

"The sun comes out," Meera answered softly.

"Exactly. Dark clouds don't mean the sun has gone forever. They only mean the sun is waiting to shine brighter. Just like that, your problems, your sadness, your failures—are only clouds. They cannot steal your sun forever."

Her words were calm, but they entered the hearts of the children like warm light seeping through cold cracks. Aarav pressed his lips together, but he felt something stir inside him—a faint warmth, a small flicker that had been buried under his pain.

Ms. Jemima placed the broken chalk on the desk in front of her. "So remember this lesson, my dear children," she said gently. "You may feel broken, you may feel weak, you may feel the world has turned its back on you. But like this chalk, you can still leave your mark. Like that bird, you can still fly. Like the sky, your sun will shine again."

The bell rang just then, shrill and sharp, but no one moved. The class remained still, as if under a spell.

"Alright," she smiled, breaking the silence, "go for your break now. And carry this lesson in your heart—not just in your notebook."

The students began to rise, murmuring among themselves, but Aarav stayed seated. For the first time in many days, his eyes held a faint glimmer, almost like the hint of dawn after a long night.

The classroom slowly emptied, the sound of footsteps and chatter fading down the corridor. Aarav remained at his desk, staring quietly at the broken chalk Ms. Jemima had left behind. His fingers rolled it between his palms as though it were something fragile, almost sacred.

"Still here, Aarav?" Ms. Jemima's soft voice came from the doorway. She had stayed behind on purpose, watching the others leave. He looked up quickly, a little startled. "Oh... yes, ma'am. I'll go." He rose halfway, clutching his notebook.

"Sit," she said gently, walking over. "No rush."

Aarav sank back into his chair. His eyes shifted nervously, as if afraid she had read all the things hidden in his heart.

Ms. Jemima pulled a chair beside him and sat, not as a teacher with authority, but as a friend who wanted to listen. For a moment she said nothing, allowing the silence to breathe. Then she nodded at the chalk in his hand.

"You kept it." He lowered his gaze. "I... I don't know why."

"Maybe because it whispered something to you," she said softly.

Aarav's lips trembled. He wanted to speak, but words felt heavy. Finally, in a voice barely above a whisper, he said, "Ma'am... sometimes I feel like that chalk. Broken. Like I can't... do anything anymore." Her heart clenched, but her face remained calm. "And yet," she said, "the chalk in your hand is still writing. Isn't it?"

He looked at her, eyes moist. "But... what if I never feel whole again?"

Ms. Jemima leaned closer, her voice steady. "Aarav, nobody in this world is perfectly whole. Every person carries cracks. Do you know what makes pottery in Japan special?" He shook his head faintly.

"It's called Kintsugi," she explained. "When a bowl breaks, they don't throw it away. They repair it with gold. The cracks remain, but they shine even brighter. That's what makes it precious."

Aarav swallowed hard. "But what if the cracks hurt too much?"

She nodded, understanding. "They do, Aarav. Pain doesn't vanish in one day. But pain doesn't define you—it shapes you. The cracks may hurt, but they will also make you stronger, more compassionate, more real. Like the bowl, you too can shine through your scars."

He looked at her, blinking back tears. "Ma'am... sometimes I feel so alone. Like no one understands."

Her eyes softened.
"You are not alone, Aarav. Not in this classroom, not in life. Look around you—you have friends, teachers, family. Even when it feels like the world is empty, there is always someone waiting to hold your hand. And when you think there's no one—remember this moment. Remember me. I am here for you. Your parents are your best friends ever to listen to all your anguish."

Aarav's throat tensed. He allowed a tear to escape, sliding down his cheek. He quickly wiped it away, embarrassed.

But Ms. Jemima smiled gently. "Tears are not weakness, Aarav. They are proof you're alive, proof your heart still cares."

He let out a shaky breath, almost a half-smile. "You really think... I can still fly? Like the bird you said?"

She placed her hand lightly on his shoulder. "I don't just think, Aarav. I know. I am confident. The sky is waiting for you, my boy."

A silence followed—warm, not heavy. Aarav felt the fog in his chest begin to clear, just a little.

He whispered, almost to himself, "Maybe... maybe I can try again."

"That's all life ever asks," Ms. Jemima said gently. "Just try."

"Remember, it's okay to feel lost. Even storms pass, and you're stronger than you think."

"Strong? Me? I'm a wreck, I think. An unavoidable disaster."

"Maybe... but look at you. You're still here. You survived anger, despair, and silent screams. That's strength." She moved out of the classroom then.

"Maybe she's right. Maybe being alive despite all this is... strength." He uttered.

He remembered Ms. Jemima from last year, encouraging him after a failed test. She had said, "Failure is a step toward understanding, not the end." He had dismissed it then, thinking it was cliché. But today, it resonated differently.

"Maybe people can see what we can't see in ourselves," he whispered.

Back in his room in late night, Aarav opened his diary. He hesitated, then wrote:
"Today, someone saw me—not my mask, not my anger, not my diary. Just me. And she reminded me... storms pass. Maybe I can survive this storm too."

He drew a small cloud with rays of light breaking through—messy but meaningful.

Below it, he noted:
"18 days left."

Lying in bed, Aarav felt something he hadn't felt in days: a flicker of hope. Not overwhelming, not certain, but subtle.

"Maybe... maybe I'm not as invisible as I thought," he whispered.

For the first time in nearly two weeks, the thought of tomorrow didn't feel like a threat. It felt... bearable.

"You are not behind—you are exactly where your journey begins."

Day 13 – Mirror Talks

"Hopelessness is a fog; it hides the horizon, not the horizon itself."

Aarav woke to a gray morning. The sunlight filtered weakly through the curtains, casting long shadows on his walls. He walked to the bathroom, yawning, and stopped before the mirror.

The reflection staring back at him looked tired, hollowed, almost unfamiliar.

"Who are you anymore?" he whispered, fingers tracing the cold surface.

"You're weak. Look at yourself. Pathetic. You cry at nothing, get angry at everything, and hide behind a mask every day."

"Is that true?" a softer voice asked, almost like it came from inside the mirror itself.

"Of course it's true. Look at all you've failed at. You're nothing."

"Or maybe... you've survived. Despite all of it, you're still here. You've felt everything, and that takes courage too."

He leaned closer, studying his own eyes. The dark circles, the red rimmed lids, the tense jaw—it all screamed despair. But beneath it, he noticed a flicker, a trace of resilience.

"Maybe she's right," he whispered, thinking of Ms. Jemima's words from yesterday. "Maybe surviving is a kind of strength."

A memory surfaced from when he was seven. He had fallen off his bicycle, scraped knees bleeding, and looked at his reflection in a puddle. His father had come over, lifted him up, and said, "You're tougher than you think, son. You just need to believe it."

He had laughed then, trying to hide the pain. Now, decades later, the reflection reminded him of that resilience buried deep inside.

"The kid in the puddle... maybe he's still in there," Aarav muttered and moved to college.

He spent his entire day in the library reading different books about great warriors of history. He just wanted to feel the struggle and challenges they faced and how they conquered them in a way that even history is glorifying their endeavor.

Aarav came back around 5 p.m. and sat with his mom. He started talking to her very lovingly and slept in her lap for a while. His mom held him firmly, as if he were a small child, and gently fingered his silky hair so that he might sleep for some time.

She woke him up around 8 p.m. by a gentle whisper:
"Wake up, Aarav. It's dinner time now. Just take you dinner and go to bed early today. No night chat! Ok."

Aarav got up lazily, washed his face, and sat down to have dinner at the dining table. After finishing that he moved straight to his room.

The room was too quiet. Too still.
Aarav sat slouched at the edge of his bed, staring into the dim ceiling light that flickered above him. Its weak light swayed in rhythm with the night breeze seeping through the half-open window. The curtain shifted, whispering against the wall like a restless soul. Somewhere outside, a dog barked once, then silence swallowed it again.

His books lay scattered on the desk, covered with a fine coat of dust. The half-finished painting in the corner leaned awkwardly against the wall, its colors dried, its story abandoned. Aarav couldn't bring himself to touch it anymore. He feared the emptiness it reminded him of.

With a sigh heavy enough to sink him deeper into the floor, Aarav rose. His bare feet dragged against the cool tiles. Step by step, he moved toward the mirror standing tall near his wardrobe. It loomed before him, waiting.

The boy in the mirror looked back, and for a moment Aarav wanted to turn away. The reflection didn't feel like him anymore. The hair was unkempt, the eyes hollow and swollen from sleepless nights. His lips were pale, his shoulders drooped. He wasn't the boy who once dreamed of sketching skies and painting stories. He looked like a ghost of that boy.

He leaned closer. The mirror fogged faintly with his breath. He spoke, barely audible, his voice coarse.

Aarav (murmuring):
"Who are you? ... Is this really me? Look at you. Tired, wasted... a stranger. You don't even resemble the boy who wanted to change the world."

His fingers lifted and pressed against the mirror. The cold glass bit at his skin, making him shiver. For a heartbeat, the reflection blurred with the faint wetness of his eyes. And then... something stirred within. A softer voice. His own voice—but gentler, warmer, almost as if the mirror were speaking back.

Mirror (calm, steady):
"Is that really all you see? Just a broken boy? Look deeper, Aarav. Those tired eyes... they carry battles fought. That spirit... it isn't shattered, only bent. And bent things can be straightened."

Aarav's lips curled into a humorless smile. A bitter laugh escaped him.

Aarav (mocking, almost laughing at himself):
"Straightened? You sound like those empty pep talks... meaningless words written on posters. Easy to say, impossible to live. Look at me! What have I achieved? Dreams shattered, promises unfulfilled. Nothing! Nothing at all!"

His voice cracked as he slammed his fist lightly against the wooden frame of the mirror. The glass quivered but held. His chest rose and fell in jagged waves. The echoes of his outburst bounced back from the walls, making the room feel smaller, tighter.

For a moment, despair threatened to choke him. But then, through his own ragged breathing, another voice surfaced—firm, like a thread of light cutting through the darkness.

Mirror (gentle but strong):
"You built survival. Isn't that something? You're still breathing, still here. Remember what Ms. Jemima said? 'Life is not measured by the days we laugh, but by the days we refuse to collapse.' You refused, Aarav. Even in pain, you refused."

The name—Ms. Jemima—lit a spark in his memory.

Suddenly, Aarav could see her again, tall and composed in front of the classroom, chalk dust on her hands, her voice ringing with a conviction that silenced even the noisiest student. Her eyes had carried that rare combination of warmth and command, and her words had burned themselves into Aarav's heart that day:

"There will be nights when hope hides itself. That's when you must become your own hope. Like a lamp in a dark room. Even a flicker is enough."

The memory made Aarav swallow hard. His hand trembled against the mirror as if trying to hold onto that flicker.

Aarav (hoarse, whispering):
"But... what if I'm too weak? What if this darkness swallows me whole before I find any light?"

His reflection looked back at him, not with judgment but with calm defiance. The gentler voice spoke again, steady as sunlight creeping under a closed door.

Mirror (encouraging):
"Darkness cannot erase light, Aarav. Meera's painting told you that truth. Do you remember? The canvas soaked in shadows—but in one corner, a single stroke of gold made the whole painting come alive. You called it beautiful. Why can't you see that same beauty in yourself?"

His chest tightened. Images of Meera's painting swam into his mind—the bold brushstrokes of black, heavy and suffocating, yet pierced by a streak of radiant yellow. That single ray had changed everything. He remembered staring at it, his heart strangely stirred, as though the painting whispered directly to him.

Aarav blinked, his tears threatening to spill.

Aarav (hesitant, voice quivering):
"So... do you think there's still... light in me? That even with these scars, these failures, I can still shine?"

For a second, his reflection seemed to soften. The lines of despair in his face looked less cruel, less permanent.

Mirror (gentle, warm):
"Not think. Know. Your scars don't hide the light, Aarav—they let it out. You are not worthless. You are unfinished. And unfinished stories often become masterpieces."

Aarav exhaled sharply, a sound halfway between a sob and relief. His shoulders, once weighed down, seemed to lift slightly. The trembling in his hands eased as he looked at himself differently—less like an enemy, more like a companion waiting to be trusted again.

His lips parted, voice firmer this time.

Aarav (soft vow):
"Then... maybe tomorrow I'll start again. Not with miracles, not with fireworks... just with small steps. For me. To prove I still matter."

The reflection mirrored his resolve, steady now. His heart thudded, not with fear, but with a fragile determination.

Mirror (soft, almost a blessing):
"You are your own ray of light, Aarav. Don't forget that."

Aarav leaned forward until his forehead touched the cold glass. The chill grounded him. A tear escaped his eye, but this time it carried no shame. It was a release. A cleansing. The silence in the room no longer felt suffocating. It felt sacred.

He closed his eyes and whispered—this time with clarity, with finality.

Aarav (steady, sure):
"I am still here. And that is enough... for now."

The ceiling light flickered once more above him. But strangely, the shadows that spread across the room didn't feel frightening anymore. They looked like a blank canvas—waiting for a new color, a new brushstroke, a new beginning.

He opened the diary. He hesitated, then wrote:
"I argued with myself in the mirror today. Harsh voice said I'm worthless. Gentle voice said I'm surviving. I don't know which is right... but maybe both are. Maybe surviving itself is proof I'm not nothing."

He drew a small outline of a face in the mirror with one half shadowed and the other lit.

Below it, he noted:
"17 days left."

Stepping back to his bed, Aarav whispered into the darkness:
"Maybe I don't have to hate myself completely. Maybe I can be angry, sad, scared... and still alive. Maybe that's enough for now."

He didn't just endure—he recognized that endurance itself could be the beginning of understanding himself.

"Even if you can't see it yet, the sun still rises tomorrow."

Day 14 – First Spark of Hope

"Kindness toward others begins with kindness toward yourself."

The morning was quiet. Aarav sat by his window, staring at the world outside—a world that seemed alive yet distant, almost mocking in its indifference.

"Halfway through... 14 days gone," he muttered. "And I'm still here."

On his way to college, Aarav noticed an old man struggling to carry groceries across the street. Without thinking, Aarav stepped forward to help.

"Thank you, young man," the old man said, smiling kindly. "Kindness is rare these days. Keep it alive."

For some reason, the words hit harder than he expected. It wasn't just gratitude—it was recognition, human connection, a reminder that small actions mattered.

"Maybe... maybe life isn't completely hollow," Aarav whispered to himself.

"Don't get carried away. One good act doesn't erase all the pain."

“Maybe not. But it’s something. A flicker. A spark.”

“A spark... it’s too little. You’ll need more to survive.”

“Maybe this is the start. One spark is enough to begin noticing more.”

Aarav remembered being eight, chasing fireflies in the backyard with his sister. The lights flickered in the dark, tiny, fragile, yet mesmerizing. He had been enchanted then, staring at them in awe.

"Life is like fireflies... fragile, fleeting, but sometimes magical," he whispered. “Maybe I forgot to look for the magic.”

He felt bit hungry so moved to cafeteria for some snacks. The cafeteria smelled of warm bread and strong coffee, the kind that reminded Aarav of Saturday mornings back home, when life felt slow and predictable. He pushed the door open, letting a sliver of autumn sunlight fall across the worn wooden floor. The faint clatter of plates and low murmur of conversation filled the air, but Aarav moved as if through a fog. It had been one of those weeks where nothing seemed to go right—rank lost, deadlines looming, and the persistent ache of exhaustion gnawing at him.

“Morning, Aarav! The usual?” called out Mrs. D’Souza from behind the counter, her apron dusted with flour.

The “usual” meant a black coffee and a sandwich. Predictable, comforting—the same comfort he had been missing in life lately. He hesitated for a fraction of a second, then nodded. “Yeah... thanks, Mrs. D’Souza.”

She handed him the coffee first, then the sandwich, steam rising gently from the warm bread. For a moment, Aarav just stood there, letting the aroma anchor him. It was ordinary, yet grounding—the kind of small pleasure he had long ignored.

"You look tired, Aarav. Long week?" Mrs. D'Souza asked, leaning slightly forward, her eyes soft behind her glasses. There was no judgment, no hollow sympathy—just a steady warmth that made him feel, strangely, like he could breathe.

"You could say that," he said, his voice dry. "Feels like everything's going wrong at once."

She nodded knowingly, as if she had heard this from every soul who walked through her doors. "I know a little trick. When things feel heavy, sometimes you just need to notice one small good thing. One little thing that's yours today."

Aarav blinked. "Like... what?"

She pointed to the sandwich. "Right here. Fresh bread. Crispy outside, soft inside. No one else can taste it like you do." She gave a small wink. "And this coffee—perfect temperature. Take ten minutes, just ten, and enjoy it. Forget everything else for a little while."

Aarav looked at the sandwich, at the soft golden crust, the slight gloss of butter melted into it. It wasn't magical. It wasn't going to fix the stress, the endless responsibilities. But... he could taste it. Really taste it. The warmth of the bread, the tang of mustard, the way the coffee steamed against his lips—it was ordinary, yet enough to make him pause.

He chuckled quietly. "You make it sound like life's secret is a sandwich."

Mrs. D'Souza's laugh was gentle, melodic. "Sometimes it is. Sometimes a small thing is enough to remind you there's still good around, even if it's tiny."

Aarav nodded slowly, feeling a spark in his chest—not fireworks, not a sudden miracle—but something steadier, quieter. A little anchor. A reminder that life had small pieces worth noticing, and maybe that was enough to keep going, just for today.

He moved to a corner table, carefully balancing his tray. As he walked, he noticed a student drop a notebook. Without thinking, he picked it up and handed it back.

"Here, you dropped this," he said.
"Thanks!" the student replied with a bright, unburdened smile before returning to their table. Aarav felt a small warmth inside—an ordinary, human exchange that made him feel connected, just a little.

Sitting down, he unwrapped the sandwich slowly, letting each layer of flavor remind him of something he could control: the present moment. He noticed the faint smell of coffee from a table nearby, the murmur of conversations, the scratch of chairs against the floor. Each sound, each smell, each movement was ordinary—but it reminded him that the world still existed outside the chaos he carried.

"Rough week?" a voice asked from the next table.

Aarav looked up. A woman, maybe a nurse or student, was packing her lunch bag. She had a tired smile, but her eyes held understanding.

"Something like that," Aarav admitted.

She nodded. "I know the feeling. But sometimes you just need one small thing to remind you it's worth continuing. For me, it's this coffee." She gestured to her cup. "Even if nothing else works, I make sure I take a sip slowly. That one moment is mine."

Aarav smiled faintly. "Yeah... I think I understand that."
After so many days, he allowed himself to linger on something simple. Not on the missed deadlines, not on the studies which had worsened, not on the endless worries. Just the warmth in his hands, the taste of food, the presence of people who noticed each other in small ways.

Mrs. D'Souza walked by, clearing a tray. "How's it going over here, Aarav?"

"Better," he said softly. "Thanks."

She nodded, giving him a brief, knowing look before moving on. And that was enough—a quiet reassurance that he wasn't invisible, that someone cared in some small way.

Aarav finished his coffee slowly, savoring the final sip. He realized the spark of hope wasn't dramatic or sudden. It wasn't a life-altering event. It was noticing something familiar, ordinary, and entirely his own. Something he could carry beyond the cafeteria door—a small, steady flame that reminded him even on hard days, he could find little pieces of life worth holding onto.

As he left the cafeteria, he felt lighter—not free from the troubles ahead, but ready to face them, one step at a time. The spark wasn't big, but it was enough. It was enough to make him believe that maybe, just maybe, tomorrow could feel a little easier.

Back in his room in evening, Aarav opened his diary. His pen hesitated over the page, then began to flow:

"Today... a spark. Not a flame, not a light that blinds, just a tiny flicker. But it reminds me... life still exists beyond the pain. Maybe I can notice it."

He drew a small flickering flame beside the words.

Below it, he added:
"16 days left."

Before sleeping, Aarav whispered softly, almost afraid to hope:
"Maybe... just maybe... there's a reason to stay alive for tomorrow."

For the first time in two weeks, the thought of tomorrow carried a gentle curiosity instead of dread.

Aarav experiences a conscious recognition that life still holds small moments of meaning, a turning point in his journey.

"Forgive yourself for the days you only survive."

Day 15 – The Dilemma

"Every heartbeat is a reminder—you are still here."

Aarav woke to the soft hum of the morning, the sunlight streaming weakly through the blinds. Sitting on his bed, he held his diary close, staring at the pages filled with fourteen days of despair, small sparks, and silent confessions.

"Halfway through..." he whispered.

He opened the diary to a blank page and began listing, almost like weighing two scales in his mind:

Reasons to Die:

-Pain never fully goes away.

-I feel invisible to everyone.

-I have failed in so many ways.

Reasons to Live:

-Small sparks of hope exist.

-Acts of kindness matter.

-I'm still breathing... still surviving.

He paused, staring at the uneven lists. The "reasons to die" were heavy, loud, almost screaming. The "reasons to live" were faint, fragile, but undeniable.
"Look at these reasons... your pain is real, your despair is real."

"And these reasons to live... they're so small. Tiny flickers."

"Maybe a flicker is enough. Maybe all life needs is a spark to begin again."

"Or maybe it's just an illusion. A cruel trick."

Aarav's hands trembled. He wanted clarity, certainty, an answer. But life never gave that. All it offered were choices, messy and ambiguous.

He remembered being sixteen, standing at a literal crossroads in his neighborhood. He wanted to run away from his problems, choosing one street to escape. His father had appeared, hand on his shoulder, and said quietly:

"Life is made of crossroads, Aarav. You won't always know the right path, but moving forward is the only way to see."

The memory felt alive again. The crossroads were still there, metaphorically, in every day since.

"Maybe the crossroads are still here," he muttered, tracing the lines in his diary.

Aarav walked to nearby park for some change and sat alone at the far corner of the small public park bench. The weather was very cool, calm and soothing. Light breeze of air on his face was giving him feel of someone with him. The sun mingled with clouds, was throwing patches of yellow light on the cracked pavement. His hands were clenched together so tightly his knuckles had turned white. Inside his head, two voices wrestled like predators fighting over the same prey.

One voice whispered:
"What's the point, Aarav? Nothing changes. You try, you fail. People don't really care. You're just dragging yourself from one empty day to another."

The other voice, calmer but firmer, spoke back:
"And yet, you're still here. You've survived every other day you thought would break you. Isn't that proof you can keep going?"

Aarav shut his eyes, trying to breathe. The practical part of him—the one that always solved problems, that told his younger sister to do her homework and his parents not to worry—rose up inside.

"If life is unbearable," it reasoned coldly, "isn't stopping it just another solution?"

But then another part countered:
"Is it a solution—or an escape? If you end it, you end the possibility of change. You end the chance to feel something different. You never know what could be waiting for you."

He thought about the faces of people he loved. His mother, who still left his favorite food on the kitchen counter. His little sister, who called him for help with math problems. Mrs. D'souza from the cafeteria, who always slipped an extra sandwich on his plate with a warm, "You look tired, son. Eat more."

And suddenly he felt the weight of what his leaving would do to them.
"Would they cry? Would they blame themselves? Or would they move on, thinking I was weak?"

Aarav's chest tightened. It wasn't just about his pain anymore. It was about the echo of his absence.

He opened his phone and scrolled through his notes. There was a single line he'd written weeks ago after reading an article:

"Suicide is a permanent solution to a temporary problem."

The practical side of his mind latched on to that. "Temporary problem," it repeated. "You've solved hard problems before. This is just another one. Maybe not today, maybe not tomorrow, but there's always a possibility you haven't tried yet."

Tears stung his eyes. "But I'm tired," he whispered under his breath. "So tired of fighting."

The calmer voice didn't sugarcoat it:
"You are tired. That's true. But resting isn't quitting. You don't have to be perfect or happy right now. You just have to stay. One more hour. One more day. Until the tiredness fades."

Aarav rushed back to his room and threw himself in bed. The ceiling fan creaked in a slow, uneven rhythm – the only sound in the room. Aarav lay on his bed, staring blankly at the shadows that the fan's blades cast on the wall. His body was still, but his mind... his mind was a restless battlefield. Dilemma in thoughts was on peak.

"What am I even doing?" he thought. "Waking up every day just to pretend I'm fine? Smiling so that others don't ask questions I can't answer?"

His chest tightened. There was no clear sadness, no specific reason, just an ache — a dull, heavy ache that followed him everywhere.

Then the first voice spoke, the cold, rational one that always appeared when emotions got too loud:
"Let's think practically, Aarav. You've tried, haven't you? You've studied, you've worked hard, you've adjusted, you've smiled when you didn't want to. But has anything changed?"

He swallowed hard. "No... not really."

The voice continued:
"Then what's the point? People move on anyway. You disappear, the world doesn't stop spinning. Maybe this pain finally ends if you stop existing. Maybe that's peace."

Aarav's pulse quickened. His hands trembled slightly. He sat up, staring into the dark. His breath grew shallow.

"Peace..." he repeated in his head, "or just nothingness? Is that really peace, or just absence?"

Then, from somewhere deeper — softer, more human — another thought broke through:
"You're assuming the pain is permanent. But have you ever waited long enough to see if it changes?"

He shook his head, arguing with himself. "I've waited for years. It's the same emptiness."

"No," the gentler voice reasoned, "it's not the same. It comes in waves. Sometimes smaller, sometimes larger. It always hurts, but you survive every time. That means something."

He stared at the dim light filtering through the curtain. "Maybe I survive because I'm too scared to die."

"Or maybe," the other voice whispered, "because there's still a part of you that wants to live."

That sentence lingered. He felt it in his chest – not comforting, but grounding. His mind jumped again – restless, logical, desperate for answers:
"If life is just endless struggle, isn't ending it the rational choice? Why keep doing something that brings pain?"

"Because not every day will be this painful," the voice replied, almost pleading. "You know that. You've had moments – even small ones – where you laughed, where you felt something real. Mrs. D'souza handing you that extra piece of sandwich. The way your sister hugged you after her exam. Those moments don't fix everything, but they prove something still matters."

He pressed his palms against his face. Tears threatened, but he didn't let them fall. His breathing was uneven.

"But I'm tired," he thought. "Tired of pretending, tired of hoping."

"Then rest," the inner voice said. "Rest, don't quit. You don't have to have answers tonight. Just breathe. Let the world be blurry for a while. You don't need to figure out the meaning of life when you're this exhausted."

Aarav looked around the room – the books, the mug with unfinished tea, the half-written note on his desk that said "Maybe tomorrow will be better."

He let out a shaky sigh. His anxiety still coiled tightly inside him, his heart still heavy, but somewhere in that chaos, a small decision surfaced:
He didn't know how to live – but he would not stop trying tonight.

Aarav stared at the night sky. The stars weren't many, but a few flickered faintly. He realized that even faint light could survive the darkness. He wiped his face with the back of his hand. The dilemma wasn't gone, but the decision—at least for tonight—was:
He would stay.

Aarav opened his diary and wrote:
"Today, I confronted the dilemma. The reasons to die shout louder, but the reasons to live... they exist. Maybe life is a choice every day. And maybe, for today, I choose to live—just to see what happens next."

He drew a small scale, uneven, with one side heavier than the other, but balanced in the center by a tiny spark.

Below it, he added:
"15 days left."

Before sleeping, he whispered into the darkness:
"I don't know what the future holds... but for now, I'll choose to stay. Just today. One day at a time."

The choice felt active—not forced, not imposed—but genuinely his. Aarav consciously weighs his reasons to live and die, marking a pivotal midpoint in his journey toward self-discovery and hope.

"Being alive is already an act of defiance against despair."

Day 16 – A Conversation with a Friend

"You cannot control the waves, but you can learn to ride them."

The morning sun spilled through the classroom windows, warming the desks and the scattered papers. Aarav sat quietly, half-listening to the lecture, half-lost in thought.

"15 days gone... and somehow I'm alive," he whispered.

During the break, Rahul—his old friend from childhood—walked over.

"Hey Aarav, you've been quiet lately. Everything okay?" he asked, genuinely concerned.

Aarav's heart thumped. Nobody had asked him like this in a long time. For a moment, he hesitated. The mask was heavy, but something in Rahul's eyes invited honesty.

Finally, he said softly, "I... I've been struggling."

Rahul sat down beside him. "You know you can tell me anything, right? I'm here."

Aarav's voice was shaky at first, but words began to flow:
"It's like... the world is heavy, and no one notices. I try to smile, I try to be normal... but inside... it's chaos."

Rahul nodded, listening without judgment. "I get it. Life can be crushing. But you don't have to go through it alone. You're not invisible to me."

Aarav: (rubbing his cold hands absently) You know, sometimes I feel like I'm just... existing. Like, everything's on repeat. Same classes, same faces, same pressure. Nothing makes sense anymore.

Rahul: (grins) Bro, you sound like you've been watching too much philosophical YouTube at night.

Aarav: (sighs) I'm not joking, dear. It's like my brain's always heavy. Even when I'm laughing with everyone, inside it just feels... empty.

Rahul: Hmm... so basically, system crashed. Bro, I think you need a reboot.

Aarav: Reboot? How do I do that? There's no "refresh" button on me, dude.

Rahul: (snaps fingers) There is! It's called life outside your head. You've been thinking too much, overloading your brain like Chrome with 50 tabs open. Close a few!

Aarav: (smirks faintly) Trust you to make therapy sound like tech support.

Rahul: Exactly. That's what I am—your mental tech support. Step one: uninstall overthinking. Step two: install good vibes only.

Aarav: And where do I download those from?

Rahul: From me, obviously. Premium subscription, no ads.

(Aarav chuckles softly.) "You're a clown, bro.

Rahul: Yes, but I'm your clown. And seriously, I get it. Everyone hits that phase where life feels like a bad Wi-Fi connection. You keep trying to reconnect, but it keeps saying "No Internet."

Aarav: (laughs more openly now) Dude, that's actually accurate.

Rahul: So, here's what we'll do. Tonight—no sulking, no scrolling Insta. We're going for a night drive. Windows down, music loud, and we'll scream old jazz songs till our throats die.

Aarav: Night drive? You serious?

Rahul: Dead serious. And after that, we're hitting Sharma tea stall for strong tea and butter toast. Real therapy session.

Aarav: Bro... I actually miss those late-night butter toast talks. That used to be our vibe.

Rahul: Exactly! You've gone too "serious mode" lately. Life's not an exam paper, bro. You don't have to get all the answers right.

Aarav: Hmm... maybe I just needed someone to say that. Everything's been feeling too heavy, you know?

Rahul: That's why I'm here. You can dump your emotional baggage anytime, but next time at least bring snacks, okay? Listening burns calories.

Aarav: (laughs and shakes his head) You're such an idiot.

Rahul: Idiot? Maybe. But a wise idiot.

(Rahul suddenly takes a french fry and flicks it at Aarav. It hits him on the shoulder.)

Aarav: Ohh! What the—?

Rahul: You were being too serious again. Fry therapy, bro. Works faster than antidepressants.

Aarav: (grinning now) You're gonna regret that.

(Aarav picks up a piece of paper napkin, rolls it, and throws it back. It hits Rahul on the forehead. Both burst out laughing like kids.)

Rahul: Okay, okay, enough! People are staring, bro. They'll think we've lost it.

Aarav: (still laughing) Maybe we already had!

Rahul: Perfect. Then let's go all in. Come, we'll bunk the next lecture and hit the football ground. Let's do something stupid again—for old times' sake.

Aarav: You sure you're not just trying to skip class?

Rahul: Absolutely. But this time, I'll call it "mental health break." Sounds fancier, right?

Aarav: (finally smiling genuinely) Yeah... maybe I needed that too—a break. From everything.

Rahul: Then it's decided. Tonight we live a little. Tomorrow we figure stuff out. Deal?

Aarav: Deal.
(They bump fists. Aarav's eyes look lighter now. He feels a spark of warmth—small, but real. Rahul went to his way.)

After a long time, Aarav felt seen—not as the smiling mask, not as a diary of silent screams, but as himself.
"This... feels strange. Relief? Connection?"
"It's okay to feel that. Feeling doesn't make you weak. It makes you human."
"Maybe... maybe people can matter after all."
He remembered sitting under a tree with Rahul at age ten, sharing secrets, making promises. They had laughed until their stomachs hurt, believing nothing could touch them.

"I forgot how it feels to be heard... really heard," he whispered.
Back in his room, Aarav opened his diary:
"Today, I talked to Rahul. Not just small talk... really talked. And I realized... maybe sharing pain doesn't make it heavier. Maybe it makes it lighter."

He drew two stick figures side by side, smiling, connected by a small line.
Below it, he added:
"14 days left."

Aarav uttered softly to himself:
"Maybe... there are people who see me. Maybe I don't have to carry this alone anymore."
For the first time in over two weeks, connection felt like a tangible lifeline rather than a fleeting illusion.
He quietly closed his eyes and said to himself,:
"Sharing is caring, very well said. You can't be always correct in your thoughts and decisions. You need someone to filter the ideas for you. Rahul my buddy...thank you for being with me."

"Today, you floated. Tomorrow, you may swim."

Day 17 – Small Victories

"The darkest nights give birth to the brightest stars."

The morning was clouded. Birds chirped cheerfully outside, and the gentle aroma of freshly brewed coffee filled the air. Aarav stretched lazily, a smile tugging at his lips as he heard his mom humming an old tune in the kitchen. The clink of cups, the sizzle of butter on toast, and the warmth of the rising day made everything feel light, new, and full of promise. It was one of those mornings where even the simplest things—sunshine, music, and laughter—felt like quiet blessings.

The sun was still shy, peeping from behind the old tree when Aarav tied his shoelaces. The early chill brushed against his face as he stepped out for his morning jog. For weeks he had been trying to wake up early, but his body often betrayed his will.
Today, though, was different. He smiled – "At least I made it before sunrise."
A small victory, but it felt like reclaiming a piece of himself.

As his feet thumped gently on the pavement, he noticed the familiar faces – the old man with his radio, the milkman balancing crates, the group of teenagers laughing over something silly. A stray puppy ran beside him for a while, tongue out, tail wagging. Aarav laughed, breathless but cheerful. By the time he finished his jog and stretched near the park bench, his smart watch blinked: 3.5 km – his best yet.
"Consistency beats perfection," he whispered, recalling a quote he had read somewhere.

Back home, he made himself a cup of lemon water instead of skipping straight to coffee – another tiny win. His mother noticed and smiled.
“Discipline suits you, son,” she said teasingly, handing him a plate of roasted cashews.
He chuckled, “I’m trying to be my better self, Mom – one morning at a time.”

After a quick shower, he prepared himself for college and felt a quiet determination as he picked up his notebook.

"Maybe today I can do something... small, but mine," he whispered.

Aarav arrived early and sat in the library with his laptop. Today, he resolved to finish a pending assignment–a task he had been postponing for weeks. Normally, the sight of endless cells in Excel would make him sigh, but today he felt different – calmer, lighter. He set a timer for one hour and focused deeply.
When the alarm buzzed, the report was done – cleaner than usual. He allowed himself a grin. “Maybe momentum is real after all.”

Hours passed. Pen scratched paper. His focus was broken by his racing thoughts, but he persisted.

Finally, he looked at the completed page and felt a strange, unfamiliar warmth.

"I did it... I actually finished something," he whispered, a faint smile tugging at his lips.

“It’s just an assignment. Small, meaningless.”

“Maybe. But it’s yours. You started it, you finished it. That matters.”

“It feels... good. Different. Not heavy. Not painful.”

“Exactly. This is the beginning of noticing the little victories.”

Around noon, he went out to the local café — Mrs. D’souza’s Cafeteria, his favorite corner spot. She greeted him warmly,

“Good morning, Mr. Early Bird! You look charged up today.”

He laughed, “Trying to earn my breakfast, Mrs. D’souza.”
She served him his usual — brown bread toast and a steaming cup of filter coffee. The first sip felt like a quiet reward.

He noticed an old poster on the wall: “Hope isn’t a miracle. It’s a muscle.”
It resonated deeply. Perhaps that’s what today was — a day of exercising hope.
In the evening, he visited the small community library where he often volunteered. The librarian, a kind old lady, waved at him.
“You came on time today, Aarav! I was wondering if the jog wore you out.”
He chuckled. “Not this time. I’ve started enjoying showing up.”

He rearranged some shelves, helped a few kids pick storybooks, and spent the last fifteen minutes reading a page from The Alchemist.
The line he stopped at read: “Every blessing ignored becomes a curse.”

He closed the book slowly, feeling the weight of gratitude in that moment.

As night fell, Aarav stood on the terrace, watching the city lights blink like scattered dreams. It wasn't a grand day – no promotions, no applause, no milestones.
But it was a day full of small successes – waking up early, finishing a task, helping someone, showing up.
He smiled to himself, whispering softly,
"Maybe joy doesn't always come from winning big... Sometimes, it's in the quiet moments when the day simply smiles back."

Back in his room, Aarav wrote in his diary:
"Today, I finished something I had been avoiding for weeks. Small, but mine. I realized... little victories can be powerful. They remind me that I'm capable, that I'm still here, and that life isn't only pain."

He drew a tiny trophy beside the entry, messy but meaningful.

Below it, he added:
"13 days left."

Aarav whispered into the quiet:
"Maybe life doesn't have to change all at once. Maybe noticing the small victories... is enough to start."

And that night, he didn't feel crushed by the weight of his entire life. One small achievement had created a space for hope. As he slipped into sleep, the faint rhythm of the morning jog still echoed in his mind – steady, hopeful, alive.

"Your light may be small now, but it is still light."

Day 18 – Breaking Patterns

“Resilience is not never falling—it is rising again each time.”

The morning light seeped softly through Aarav’s curtains. He sat at his desk, diary open, pen in hand, hesitating. Today, he decided to confront something he had done for years—staying in bed for hours, hiding from life, letting despair dictate his every move.

"Maybe today I can do it differently," he whispered.

He started challenging his habits. Instead of scrolling mindlessly through his phone, Aarav got up, dressed, and went for a short walk. The air was cool, carrying the faint scent of wet earth from last night’s rain. Every step felt deliberate, like breaking a chain that had held him captive for years.

"It’s just a walk," he thought. “But it feels... like reclaiming a little control.”

“You’ve done this your whole life... hiding, avoiding, giving up before even trying.”

“Maybe. But today I didn’t. Today, I tried.”

“One day won’t change anything.”

“No... but maybe one day is enough to start.”

He remembered mornings when he used to wake early to help his mother make breakfast or play with his sister. The routine had made him feel useful and connected. He realized that he had abandoned those small rituals over the years, sinking into patterns of avoidance and despair.

"Maybe it’s time to bring them back... slowly," he whispered.

The soft hum of the ceiling fan above doing little to soothe the storm inside his head. Thoughts of failures, missed opportunities, and imagined criticisms swirled relentlessly. Every plan he had made in the past seemed to dissolve into ashes before it even began. “Why even try?” he muttered to himself, the words tasting bitter on his tongue.

But today was different. Somehow, the words Mrs. D’souza had spoken in the cafeteria kept echoing in his mind: “You don’t have to be trapped by your thoughts, Aarav. One small shift, one tiny step, can change the way your whole day feels.”

At first, he had shrugged it off. How could one small step change anything? But as he sat in silence now, he realized that his patterns of negativity weren’t unbreakable walls—they were more like cracks in a dry pond, waiting for a stream of water to seep in.

He picked up his notebook, the one he had abandoned weeks ago. Flipping to a blank page, he hesitated. For years, every attempt at writing down his thoughts had ended in frustration, his words twisted by his own judgment. But today, he forced himself to begin.

“I will write down one good thing that happened today,” he whispered, almost laughing at how absurd it felt.

The words came slowly at first:
"The sun was warm on my face during lunch. Mrs. D'souza smiled at me. The cafeteria sandwich was better than yesterday."

Small, almost trivial things. But as he wrote, a strange sense of lightness spread through him. He realized he had been training his mind to notice only what went wrong. Why not notice what went right, however small?

He tried something new. He deliberately interrupted his spiraling thoughts. When a wave of self-doubt crept in before his class, he took a deep breath, leaned back in his chair, and repeated to himself:
"This is just a thought. It does not define me."

The thought persisted for a moment, stubborn as a shadow, but it began to lose its power.

Later, during the lunch break, Aarav surprised himself. Instead of sitting alone, he joined a small group in the cafeteria. He didn't force laughter or pretend to be someone he wasn't; he simply listened and shared tiny observations. The world outside his head seemed brighter, more immediate. Negativity, he realized, had thrived in isolation, and even small connections could shrink its grip.

By the end of the day, a subtle shift had begun. Aarav still had his low moments—old patterns don't vanish overnight—but each time he caught himself sinking into pessimism, he paused, noted the thought, and challenged it.
"Is this thought helping me, or just replaying old fears?"

Slowly, deliberately, he began to answer:
"No. It's not helping. I can try again tomorrow."

It wasn't magic. It wasn't sudden. But after a long time, Aarav felt a crack of hope in the concrete walls of his mind. And he knew, quietly, that hope was something he could build, day by day, word by word, thought by thought.

Aarav opened his drawer, took his diary, and started writing:

"Today, I broke the habit of hiding in bed and ignoring life. I went for a walk, felt the air, moved my body... and it felt like breaking a chain I didn't know I carried. Maybe changing patterns is the first step toward changing myself."

He drew a small chain with one broken link beside the entry.

Below it, he added:
"12 days left."

"Maybe I can't change everything at once... but I can change one small thing. And one small thing can matter. Breaking a negative pattern felt powerful, like I had begun reclaiming my life, one choice at a time." Aarav whispered.

"Today you rose, even if shakily. That is enough."

Day 19 – Connection Beyond Words

"Our wounds are often where compassion grows."

The morning light was soft, diffused through thin clouds. Aarav felt heavier than usual, a quiet restlessness pressing against his chest. He dragged himself to college, head down, heart weighed with thoughts he could not share.

"Maybe today is just another day... nothing changes," he whispered.

During lunch, Aarav noticed a stray dog sitting by the steps of the campus canteen. Its fur was matted, its eyes wary but gentle. Most students ignored it, laughing and pointing from a distance.

Aarav, on impulse, knelt down. The dog didn't bark or shy away—it just looked at him, tail wagging faintly, ears alert.

Without speaking, he offered a piece of his sandwich. The dog took it carefully, then leaned into him for a quiet nuzzle. It was a simple gesture. No words, no explanations. Just trust, acknowledgment, and presence.
"Why does this feel... so much?" Aarav whispered, chest tightening.

"It's just a dog. It's not human."

“Maybe... but it sees me. It trusts me. That counts for something.”

“It’s fleeting. Don’t get attached.”

“Or maybe this is exactly what I needed—a connection without judgment, without expectation.”

He remembered nights when his sister would sit beside him silently while he cried. No words, just presence. He had felt understood then, without anyone saying anything.

"Maybe this is the same... a reminder that presence alone can heal," he thought.

Aarav came back to home early with these mingled thoughts and recklessly sank in sofa.

The house was unusually quiet that afternoon. The kind of quiet that made even the ticking clock sound louder. Sunlight slipped through the curtains in soft, golden ribbons, spreading across the kitchen counter where steam from a freshly brewed cup of tea curled lazily into the air.

“Hey Aarav! How did you come so early?” Mother turned back and said.
Aarav grinned only and stepped to the dining table, sat near her, slouched over his laptop, pretending to read something important. But his eyes weren’t moving. His thoughts were elsewhere—tangled, restless, and heavy.

Life had been running too fast lately — assignments, deadlines, expectations, that endless feeling of being almost enough but not quite. And somewhere in that noise, he had lost the calm he once carried so easily.

From behind the counter came the gentle clatter of utensils and the faint humming of an old tune. His mother's voice – soft, untrained, but comforting – filled the kitchen like sunlight. It was the same song she'd been humming since he was a child. Somehow, it always made the world seem a little less complicated.

She turned slightly, noticing the faraway look on his face.
"You haven't eaten anything since morning," she said, wiping her hands on her apron.

"Coffee won't fix everything, you know."

Aarav smiled weakly. "Neither will food, Mom."

She raised an eyebrow, amused. "Spoken like someone who's forgotten how powerful my stuffed breads are."

He chuckled, despite himself. "I could never forget that."

She smiled, and for a moment, the silence between them softened.

His mother plated some fresh stuffed breads, the smell filling the air with a warmth that only home-cooked food could bring. She placed them before him with a side of mango pickle and said"
"Eat first. Then think about your crisis."

Aarav looked up. "How do you always know what's going on?"

"I'm your mother," she replied simply. "You wear your mood on your face like a breaking news."

He sighed, picking at the edge of the bread.
"It's just... nothing feels right lately. I don't even know what I'm chasing anymore."

She pulled out the chair beside him and sat down, folding her hands on the table. Her eyes – tired but kind – studied him quietly.
"You don't have to have it all figured out, my champ. Even I don't."

Aarav looked at her, surprised.
"You? But you always seem so... steady."

She laughed softly. "That's the trick of age. You learn to hide the tremors inside."

For a moment, neither spoke. Only the faint sound of boiling milk filled the silence.
Then she said:
"You remember when you were little, and your kite got stuck on that mango tree?"

Aarav smiled faintly.
"And you climbed halfway up trying to get it down."

She laughed. "Exactly. I remember scolding you afterward – said you should've been more careful. But what I didn't tell you was how proud I felt, seeing how stubborn you were to fly it again the next day."

He looked down at his plate. "I'm not that stubborn anymore, Mom. I just... get tired too easily."

She placed her hand over his, warm and firm. "Then come to me more often. Let the tiredness melt in my lap."

Something shifted in him at that moment. It wasn't a grand revelation – just a quiet realization that he hadn't allowed himself to pause in a long time.

The kitchen smelled like cumin and oil; the ceiling fan spun lazily. His mother got up to pour him another cup of coffee. The sound of the coffee trickling into the cup felt oddly comforting – like an old memory finding its way back.

"Mom," he said, watching her. "Do you ever feel... stuck?"

She smiled without turning. "Every day. But then I make good cappuccino, and somehow it feels like I'm moving again."

He laughed. "That's your solution to everything, isn't it?"

"Cappuccino and love," she said, sliding the cup toward him. "You'd be surprised how many problems those two can solve."

They sipped in silence for a while. The rain outside had begun to fall lightly, pattering against the balcony railing. Aarav watched the tiny droplets race down the windowpane. The world outside seemed blurred and calm.

His mother sat beside him, not asking questions, not offering advice – just being there. That was her way. She believed in presence more than persuasion.

Finally, she said quietly, "You know, I used to worry that you'd forget how to talk to me once you grew up."

He looked up, startled. "Why would you think that?"

"Because children stop talking when they start hiding," she said softly.
"But you don't have to hide from me, Aarav. Even your silence tells me everything."

Her words landed deep. He opened his mouth to speak but couldn't. His throat felt tight. How do you tell someone that you've been drifting through your own life like a stranger? That sometimes, even success feels hollow when it doesn't have a home to return to?

But he didn't need to explain. She already knew. That was the thing about mothers—they understood the pauses better than the sentences.

Aarav pushed his plate aside and leaned back, exhaling slowly. The familiar creak of the chair, the rhythm of rain, the smell of food – it all wrapped around him like an embrace.

He said quietly, "You know, I used to think the world outside was the only place to find peace."

"And now?" she asked.

"Now I think I was running away from the one place that already had it."

She smiled. "Home doesn't chase you, darling. It just waits."

Her words struck him with a kind of gentle truth that didn't need to be debated. Home wasn't walls and rooms – it was her voice, her warmth, her belief in him when he had none left for himself.

After a long pause, she spoke again, changing the subject lightly. "You should see how your father struggles with the Wi-Fi when you're not around. He keeps asking me to call you for help."

Aarav laughed, the sound breaking through the heaviness in the air. "That man refuses to learn."

"He says he's saving his brain cells for bigger things," she said, rolling her eyes.

They both laughed. And just like that, the heaviness lifted – not entirely, but enough for him to breathe freely again.

He realized then how effortlessly his mother balanced humor and healing. She never forced lessons; she let them bloom naturally in her words.

Later, as she washed the dishes, Aarav joined her, towel in hand. She looked surprised. "Since when do you help in the kitchen?"

"Since now," he said with a grin.

They stood side by side, the simple rhythm of washing and drying forming its own quiet melody. The world outside continued with its rush, but inside that kitchen, time felt slower, softer – like it was waiting for them.

"Mom," he said after a while, "I think I forgot how to be still. You do it so easily."

She looked at him, smiling faintly. "That's because I stopped trying to control everything. You'll learn that too."

He nodded, drying the last plate. "Maybe that's what I came home to learn."

She reached up and ruffled his hair, something she hadn't done since he was a boy. "You came home to remember who you are."

As evening settled, the sky turned dusky pink. His father returned from work, the house filled with the sounds of movement again – the clinking of keys, the familiar "How was your day?"

But something in Aarav had changed quietly. He smiled more. His voice was lighter. Even his thoughts seemed to have slowed down, syncing with the steady rhythm of home life.

Later, when he stepped out to the balcony, his mother joined him with another cup of coffee. They stood together, looking out at the rain-soaked street, the world glowing softly under streetlights.

He said, almost to himself, "I think I understand now, Mom."

"Understand what?" she asked, handing him the cup.

"That connection doesn't need words. It's there in how you wait, how you notice, how you care without asking."

She smiled — that quiet, knowing smile that mothers wear when their children finally see what was always in front of them. "That's love, my son. The kind that doesn't shout, doesn't demand, doesn't end."

He looked at her, really looked — at the faint lines on her face, the strength in her eyes, the patience she carried like second nature. He felt something shift again — not dramatically, but deeply.

He didn't say "thank you." He didn't need to. She already knew.

That night, on his bed, Aarav wrote in his diary:

"Today, a dog looked at me and trusted me. No words, no expectations, just a connection. It reminded me... connection doesn't always need speech. Sometimes it's just presence, acknowledgment, and trust. Maybe that's enough."

He drew a small dog beside the words, its tail curved upward like a tiny flag of hope.

He stayed for a while and again scribed-
"Home isn't where you stay. It's where you return to when the world stops making sense."

"And sometimes, the most powerful conversations happen in silence — between a mother and her child, between love and understanding."

Below it, he added:
"11 days left."

He closed the diary and smiled faintly. The storm in his mind had quieted, not because his problems had disappeared, but because he'd finally remembered what peace felt like.

It felt like home.
It felt like Mom.

Aarav uttered with dying eyes:
"Maybe life isn't only about words or understanding. Sometimes, being seen... even silently... is enough to keep going."

"The healing power of a silent, non-verbal bond, reinforcing the idea that empathy and presence can restore hope."

"One day, your survival may be someone else's hope."

Day 20 – A Challenge Accepted

"The future is not written; it waits for your pen."

The morning sun broke through the clouds, warm but soft, casting long shadows across Aarav's room. He sat on his bed, diary open, staring at the blank page.

"Today... I need to do something different," he whispered. "Something that scares me, even a little. I have to accept the challenges of my life on my own. "

In college, there was a small public speaking session—a volunteer event. Aarav had avoided it for years, terrified of speaking in front of anyone. Today, he surprised himself by signing up. As he waited for his turn, his stomach twisted, hands sweaty, heart racing. His mind screamed, "You can't do this. You'll fail. Everyone will laugh."

But then he remembered the dog yesterday, Rahul's listening ear, the small sparks of hope, and even his teacher's words.

"I've survived worse storms... maybe I can survive this too," he whispered.

"You're terrified. You'll mess up."

"Maybe. But I'll try anyway. Just try. That's enough."

"People will judge you."

"They always do. But I'm not doing this for them. I'm doing this for me."

The moment bellied loudly in his ears when the mic spoke his name. His turn came, Aarav stepped up, trembling slightly. He took a deep breath and spoke—

Good morning everyone!

Let me start with a simple question:
How many of you have faced a challenge so big that you thought, "I can't do this!"?

"Come on, be honest!" (pause, smile, look around)

"Wow... almost all of you! See? I'm not alone either. Life throws those curveballs at all of us."

Now, I want you to imagine something. Picture yourself standing at the bottom of a mountain. The peak is hidden in clouds. Your legs feel heavy, your heart is racing.

What's the first thing you want to do? Turn around and run?

Shout, "This is impossible!"? (pause, let a few audience members respond)

Exactly. That's the natural reaction. But here's the twist—victory doesn't come to those who run from the storm. Victory comes to those who face it. Every struggle you meet, every obstacle you stumble over, it's a chance to grow stronger, wiser, tougher.

Think of it as life's personal gym—except no membership fees! (audience chuckles)

Let me ask you another question:
"How many of you have failed at something and felt completely crushed?"
(pause)
"And yet, look at you—smiling, breathing, sitting here. That right there is proof—you can rise again. Every failure is a lesson disguised as hardship. Every step forward, no matter how small, is a victory in itself."

Now, let's do something together.

Repeat after me:
"I will face my challenges!" (pause for audience to repeat)

Fantastic! Again: "I will rise stronger!" (audience repeats])

One more time, with feeling: "I will never give up!" (audience repeats, claps)

That's the spirit!

Here's what I want you to remember when life tests you next:

First, embrace it. Say, "Yes, this is part of my journey." Don't fight reality; learn from it.

Second, keep your courage alive. Courage isn't the absence of fear—it's moving forward despite fear.

Third, believe in yourself. Look at your neighbor and say,
"We've got this!" (audience interaction) And finally, act. Tiny steps every day add up to mountains moved.

Think about the greats—people who lost everything, were knocked down again and again, yet rose.
Why?
Because they refused to surrender. They faced their challenges, learned from them, and conquered them. And if they could do it, so can you.

So I want everyone here to stand up—yes, stand up! (pause as audience stands)

-Feel your strength. (clinching his fist)

-Feel your courage. (joining his hands together in air)

And repeat with me: "I am unstoppable!" (audience repeats, some cheering)

Remember, victory is not only in the outcome—it's in the way you rise, again and again. Your challenges are not the end—they are the beginning of your greatest victories.

Thank you! [pause for applause]

When he finished, there was applause—not mocking, not overwhelming, just genuine. Aarav felt something shift inside—a sense of pride, a recognition that he had faced a fear and survived.

"I did it... I really did it," he whispered, heart pounding.

Everyone was smiling. Everyone was admiring his way of talk and style of speech. He was also happy today but not showing to the world about his inner cheer, just passing innocent and true smile.

Back in his room, Aarav wrote in his diary:

"Today, I faced a fear I thought would crush me. I spoke in front of people. I didn't fail. I felt... alive. Maybe courage isn't the absence of fear—it's acting despite it. And maybe I can do it again."

He drew a small figure standing on a stage, arms raised, surrounded by tiny sparks of light.

Below it, he added:
"10 days left."

Aarav smiled in the mirror and whispered into the quiet:
"Maybe strength isn't sudden or perfect. Maybe it's the little steps, the small challenges we accept, that build something real inside us."

"Today I felt a tangible sense of accomplishment-not just surviving, but actively participating in life."

"Tonight, you chose to keep writing."

Day 21 – Rediscovering Joy

"Happiness is not a destination—it is built in moments."

The morning air was crisp, filled with the scent of rain-soaked earth. Aarav walked to college, feeling the gentle warmth of the sun on his face. It was ordinary, mundane, yet today it felt... different.

"Maybe today can be lighter," he whispered.

During lunch break, Aarav's friends—Rahul and a few others—invited him to play a casual game of cricket in the courtyard. Hesitant at first, he finally agreed.

The afternoon sun was bright, spilling molten gold across the dusty playground. The faint smell of dry earth mixed with the scent of grass and sweat. Aarav tightened his grip on the bat, feeling its rough handle against his palms. Around him, his friends were already alive with laughter and noise – shouting instructions, arguing over field placements, someone blowing a whistle for fun.

The first few balls were cautious. He missed one, nicked another. His friends clapped anyway, cheering him on. Then came a perfectly pitched delivery – he swung instinctively, and the ball soared high over midwicket, landing near the boundary line. The roar that followed brought an unfiltered smile to his face.

Soon, Aarav found his rhythm. Every shot connected cleanly – drives, pulls, cuts – each stroke carrying the joy of freedom. The sound of leather meeting willow echoed across the ground. Sweat trickled down his temples, his heart raced, and his laughter came easily.

"Come on, Aarav! Let's see that old magic!"

"Bowl him out this time buddy!"

He smiled nervously. It had been years since he'd played seriously, but something about that banter, that carefree noise, stirred something deep within him. The bowler ran in with a thudding rhythm – one, two, three – and let the ball fly. Aarav swung instinctively.

Crack!

The ball sliced through the air, soaring high over the fielder's head and landing beyond the boundary. For a moment, silence – then the field erupted. Cheers burst from every corner – clapping, whistling, hoots of excitement.

Someone shouted, "What a shot, Aarav!" and another yelled, "Six! He's back!"

Aarav laughed, the sound unrestrained and free.

The game went on, and so did the noise – the rhythmic beat of the ball against the pitch, the rustle of running feet, the rise and fall of voices. Every cheer seemed to lift his spirits higher. He played fearless now – cover drives flashing through the air, quick singles, powerful pulls. Each connection between bat and ball filled him with something he hadn't felt in a long time – pure, unfiltered joy.

The ball soared, laughter erupted, the world felt chaotic but alive. Aarav ran, swung, missed, and laughed–a genuine, unforced laugh that startled him.

"I forgot... this feels good," he thought, breathless and smiling. "I forgot I could just enjoy something, with no masks, no pain."

"This is fleeting. Don't get attached."

"Maybe. But fleeting doesn't mean it isn't real. This... joy... it's mine, even if just for a moment."

"People won't understand. They'll think it's small."

"It's not small if it touches me. That's enough."

By the time the last over ended, Aarav had scored the highest runs. His teammates rushed toward him, clapping his back, tousling his hair, chanting his name. The evening sky turned a deep orange, and laughter echoed through the fading light.

As Aarav stood there, bat resting on his shoulder, breath steadying, he looked around at the smiling faces, the fluttering dust, the faint glow of the setting sun. The noise of the crowd was still in his ears – not just the sound of victory, but of belonging, of life, of rediscovered happiness. Aarav realized he wasn't rediscovering cricket – he was rediscovering joy itself.

Aarav remembered running barefoot in the rain as a child, spinning around, arms outstretched, laughing until his stomach hurt. Today's cricket game had brought a similar feeling—a tiny echo of a long-lost joy.

"Maybe happiness isn't gone... just buried under fear and despair," he whispered.

This time, Aarav wasn't chasing joy. He was standing right in the middle of it.

With immense feel of pleasure, Aarav opened in his diary and started writing with smile on his face:

"Today, I laughed freely. No masks, no pretending. Just pure joy. I forgot it could feel like this... light, warm, untethered. Maybe joy doesn't need permission—it just needs me to notice it."

He drew a small sun with rays radiating outward, messy but glowing.

Below it, he added:
"9 days left."

Aarav smiled and thought:
"Maybe life isn't only pain. Maybe moments of joy exist... and maybe I can find more if I allow myself."

The thought of tomorrow carried curiosity instead of fear—a gentle invitation to keep exploring life's possibilities.

"You gathered one moment of peace today. That is progress."

Day 22 – Facing Shadows

"Your life has chapters unwritten, and readers yet to meet."

The morning was quiet, almost eerily so. Aarav woke with some excitement and some heaviness he hadn't felt in days, a shadow of doubt creeping into his mind.

"Joy feels nice... but can it last? Or will the shadows catch me again?" he whispered.

During college, a poster caught his eye: an upcoming art exhibition featuring student work. A memory resurfaced—the time he had submitted a painting in middle school, only to have it harshly criticized by a teacher in front of everyone. He felt the familiar sting of shame and embarrassment, a shadow he thought he had left behind.

"Why does it still hurt after all these years?" Aarav murmured.
"You should stay away. Avoid it. Don't relive the shame."
"Maybe avoidance made it stronger. Maybe it's time to face it."
"And if it hurts too much? If I fail again?"
"Then at least I tried. And trying is better than running forever."

Confronting the memory, Aarav decided to visit the exhibition. Each painting he passed reminded him of the fear he once carried. When he reached the student submissions, he hesitated—then looked at a small corner where his own art from years ago had been displayed, preserved by the school as an example of early effort.

He was thrilled to see his old rough painting, which was displayed there to admire the efforts of a small boy.

He studied it: the strokes were rough, the colors awkward, but there was heart in it. And now, instead of harsh criticism, he saw admiration in the eyes of a few students quietly studying it.

"Maybe I wasn't a failure... just learning," he whispered.

Talking to himself, "You know... for so long, every brushstroke felt like a question – am I good enough? Every comment, every criticism, echoed louder than my own thoughts. But today... it's different."

"I'm standing here, looking at this painting – my painting – and I finally see what I was trying to say all along. It's not perfect, no. But it's mine."

"The college admired it. They actually admired it. And somehow, that means I can, too."

"All those doubts, all those sleepless nights... they were part of this canvas. Every shade carries a piece of me."

"I used to hide behind fear, behind what others thought I should be. But now – now I'm facing those shadows. And they don't scare me anymore."

"Because when I look at this painting, I see more than color. I see me. And for the first time... I'm proud of who that is."

He remembered his father telling him after the original criticism, "It's not about being perfect. It's about expressing yourself. Don't let anyone take that away from you."

Today, the memory felt alive. The shadows of shame began to shrink as he realized he had survived—and grown—since then. Aarav didn't just admire his painting—he admired himself, the courage it took to believe, and the journey that turned his uncertainty into art.

Aarav penned his diary:
"Today, I faced a shadow from my past—the shame, the fear, the embarrassment. It hurt, yes. But it also reminded me... I've grown, I've survived, and I can face fear without letting it define me."

"Shadows will always exist... but maybe I don't have to run from them. Maybe I can walk through them, one step at a time."

He drew a small shadowed figure with a faint light breaking through, messy but clear.

Below it, he added:
"8 days left."

Aarav confronted a lingering fear from his past and discovered that facing, rather than avoiding, painful memories can empower him and reduce their hold over his life. He felt that courage wasn't the absence of fear—it was moving forward despite it.

"Do not end the story before the surprise arrives."

Day 23 – Acts of Kindness

"Gratitude doesn't erase pain, but it softens its edges."

The morning air felt warmer than usual. Aarav woke with a quiet determination, a sense that he could do something meaningful—not grand, but real.

"Maybe today, I can make someone else's day a little lighter," he whispered.

On his way to college, Aarav noticed a janitor struggling to carry a heavy bucket of water. Without hesitation, he stepped forward.

"Here, let me help," he said, lifting one side of the bucket.

The janitor smiled, wiping sweat from his brow. "Thank you, young man. That was kind of you."

Aarav felt an unexpected warmth spread through his chest—a sense of purpose, a reminder that small gestures mattered.
"It's just a bucket. Why does it feel so... good?"
"Because you helped. Not for praise, not for recognition, just helped. That counts for something."

"Maybe kindness isn't just for others. Maybe it's for me too."

The corridor was buzzing with voices of new students – laughter, footsteps, the faint squeak of shoes on the polished floor. Aarav, walking briskly with his bag slung over one shoulder, noticed a boy struggling to balance a tall stack of books that looked ready to tumble any second.

"Hey, wait–" Aarav said quickly, reaching out just as the top two books wobbled.
The boy froze, nervous, clutching the pile too tightly.

"Got it?" Aarav smiled, steadying the books with one hand.
The fresher looked up, flustered but smiling. "Uh... thanks, big bro. These are... all for my first class. I didn't know they'd be this heavy."

Aarav chuckled. "Yeah, college doesn't tell you that in the brochure – 'Warning: Books weigh more than your confidence.'"

The fresher laughed for the first time, his shoulders relaxing. Aarav took half the books from his hands.
"Come on, I'll help you carry these. Where's your class?"

"First-year block... room 203," the fresher replied softly.
"Perfect, I'm going that way too," Aarav said, leading the way through the long corridor.

Carrying the books together, they walked in the corridor to the classroom. The student's gratitude lingered in the air, filling Aarav with an unfamiliar satisfaction. Sunlight streamed through the windows, painting golden patches on the floor.

"So," Aarav asked, glancing at him, "first day nerves?"
The fresher smiled awkwardly. "A little. I don't know anyone here. Everyone seems so... confident."

Aarav nodded. “Yeah, that’s how it looks from the outside. Trust me, half of them are just pretending. I did the same thing in my first year.”
“You?” the fresher asked, surprised. “You seem so... calm.”

Aarav laughed. “That’s just practice. I was a mess on my first day — dropped my notebook, forgot my timetable, and called my professor ‘uncle’ by mistake.”

The fresher burst into laughter. “No way!”
“True story,” Aarav grinned. “So you’re already doing better than me.”

They reached the classroom door. Aarav handed him the books gently. “Here you go. You’ll be fine. Just remember, everyone starts out lost — that’s how you learn your way.”

The fresher took the books, his eyes bright with gratitude. “Thank you, Aarav. Really. I was so nervous this morning, but... now I feel like maybe I’ll fit in.”

Aarav smiled warmly. “You already do. Welcome to college, bro.”

As Aarav turned to leave, the fresher called out, “Hey! Will I see you around?”

Aarav looked back, smiling. “Count on it.”

The fresher watched him disappear down the sunlit corridor, a quiet sense of belonging blooming in his chest — the first friendly face of a new beginning.

"Small acts... they ripple farther than I imagined," he thought.

He remembered giving his sister a drawing he had made, just to make her smile. She had hugged him tightly, and he had felt a joy stronger than any praise he had ever received.

"Maybe that joy hasn't disappeared," Aarav whispered.

Aarav took his pen boldly and wrote in his diary:

"Today, I helped others—not because I had to, but because I could. Each smile, each thank you... it reminded me that I can matter, even in small ways. And that maybe kindness can heal more than pain ever could."

He drew a series of small hearts connecting in a chain, messy but glowing.

Below it, he added:
"7 days left."

He came out on the balcony, stared at the starry sky and, muffled:
"Maybe life isn't just about surviving. Maybe it's also about creating small ripples of good, even when it feels insignificant. And maybe that's enough reason to stay."

He felt a sense of purpose not tied to himself alone, but connected to the world around him.

Aarav experienced the power of intentional kindness, realized that even small gestures could create meaningful connections and reinforce hope.

"Today's small gratitude is tomorrow's strength."

Day 24 – Revisiting Dreams

"You are not your mistakes; you are your possibilities."

The morning light felt gentle, almost encouraging. Aarav woke with a curiosity he hadn't felt in weeks.

"What did I love before all this... before the despair took over?" he whispered.
While walking to college, Aarav passed an old music shop. The display of guitars and sheet music pulled him closer. He hadn't played since school, but memories flooded back—him strumming clumsily, lost in the notes, feeling alive with each chord.
"I loved this... I really loved this," he murmured.

He picked up a small guitar in the shop, strummed a few notes, and felt the familiar thrill. The sound was awkward but alive, vibrating through him in a way that reminded him who he had been—who he could still be.
"It's just a memory. You're not good anymore."
"Maybe not. But feeling it again... it reminds me I can try. That I can still feel joy."
"What if I fail? What if it's too late?"
"Maybe it's never too late to begin again. Maybe beginning is all that matters."

It was his childhood passion to play flawless guitar. He remembered performing at a small school event, his hands trembling but heart racing with excitement. The applause, the smiles, the thrill of creating something—it had been magic.

"Maybe that magic is still inside me," he whispered.
The night had an odd stillness to it—one that seemed to breathe between the walls of Aarav's quiet room. Outside, the city moved in restless rhythm, cars hurrying, people chasing time, but within those four walls, everything had slowed down to a single heartbeat. Aarav sat by the old wooden window, the one that creaked when the wind passed through, and stared at the dim halo of a streetlamp below.

There was a time when he had believed light like that meant something—hope, direction, a promise of tomorrow. Now, it was just another glow in a city that had forgotten how to dream. He sipped his cold coffee and opened his worn notebook—its cover cracked, pages yellowed with time. It had been years since he'd touched it. The moment he did, a familiar scent of old paper and ink rose—a scent of another life.

He turned the first page. A poem stared back at him, written in uneven lines, dated March 2022. It was raw, uncertain, but alive. "When did I stop writing?" he whispered to no one. The silence replied with an ache that settled somewhere deep in his chest.

He remembered those nights when dreams were not fragile things—they were real, breathing entities. Back then, he would stay awake imagining worlds he wanted to build, journeys he wanted to take, people he wanted to meet. He had believed in the magic of becoming. But life had its way of folding those dreams neatly and tucking them away, under the weight of practicality and reason.
Dreams are luxuries, he had once told himself. And luxuries are for those who can afford to fail.

But now, as the rain began to fall outside, tapping lightly against the glass, Aarav felt something stir inside—a quiet rebellion, a whisper of that younger self who refused to live quietly. Maybe, he thought, forgetting dreams was never the problem; maybe it was forgetting the part of us that believed in them.

He leaned back, closing his eyes, letting the memories unfold—the sketchbook of a sixteen-year-old boy who wanted to be a filmmaker; the stories he wrote but never sent to publishers; the list of places he had promised to visit; the person he had promised himself to become. Each forgotten dream rose like mist from the dark corners of his mind. And with each memory, he felt something come alive that he hadn't felt in years—wonder. He realized dreams are not childish illusions. They are maps of the soul. They guide us toward our truest selves, even when we get lost in the maze of survival. Without them, life becomes a repetition of responsibilities, not an exploration of possibilities.

Aarav saw his reflection in the window—not the tired man who went to work and returned to silence, but the boy who used to see stories in sunsets and poetry in rain. He smiled faintly. Perhaps he hadn't lost that boy completely. Perhaps he had just stopped listening.

The clock struck midnight. Somewhere in the distance, a train passed—its whistle slicing through the quiet. Aarav looked at his notebook again. He picked up a pen that had long dried and replaced it with a new one. The first few words came awkwardly, hesitant, but they came.
"I dreamt once... and I will dream again."

The ink spread slowly on the page, as if reclaiming its right to exist. In that moment, he wasn't chasing success, or meaning, or redemption. He was simply remembering. And that was enough.

He realized something profound—that dreams never truly die. They wait. They linger at the edges of consciousness, patient as old friends, waiting for us to turn around and see them again. They do not fade because they are fragile; they fade because we stop believing we are worthy of them.

The rain softened, the city quieted, and Aarav felt something he hadn't felt in years—a sense of becoming. Tomorrow, he didn't know what he would do. He didn't have a plan, or a promise, or even clarity. But he had a direction. And that, he thought, is how every dream begins.

He closed the notebook, but his heart stayed open. After many weeks of struggle, Aarav wasn't afraid of time passing. He had remembered what time could not erase—the gentle pulse of a forgotten dream, still alive within him, waiting to guide him home.

He returned in his bed and wrote a note:
"Today, I revisited something I loved—music. I strummed a guitar and felt sparks of joy I thought were gone. I remembered my dreams. Maybe dreams don't vanish; maybe they wait for us to notice them again."
He drew a small guitar with a few musical notes floating upward.
Below it, he added:
"6 days left."

"Maybe life isn't only about pain and survival. Maybe it's also about rediscovering the things that make my heartbeat faster. Maybe I still have dreams worth chasing." He convinced himself in faint voice.
"At least now, I could reconnect with old passions, reignite hope, and remind myself that life can still hold possibility and joy."

"Hope grows where self-forgiveness is planted."

Day 25 – Strength in Vulnerability

"Every soul is born with purpose, even if it feels hidden."

The morning was calm, with sunlight spilling softly across Aarav's room. He woke feeling introspective, aware that the past days had brought him closer to himself—but also that some walls remained. "Maybe today I can face them... not with anger, not with fear, but with openness," he whispered.

During college, Aarav's psychology class required sharing a personal experience in a group discussion. His heart raced as he realized this was a challenge—a deliberate act of exposing his inner thoughts.
When it was his turn, he took a deep breath and spoke quietly:
"I've struggled... with sadness, anger, feeling invisible. I didn't want anyone to notice, but I think hiding it has made it worse."

Silence filled the room for a heartbeat. Then, a few students nodded. One shared,
"I've felt that too. You're not alone."

Aarav felt something shift inside—relief, recognition, and a strange warmth. The act of being open had not weakened him; it had connected him to others.

"I exposed my pain. I could have been judged, laughed at..."

"Or you could have been understood. And you were. That's real strength."

"Vulnerability doesn't make me weak. It makes me human. Maybe it even makes me braver."

"Strength in Vulnerability" is one of the most powerful and misunderstood truths about human nature."

"We often think of strength as stoicism – being unshaken, invincible, and always in control. But real strength often shows itself when we dare to be open, honest, and human. Vulnerability isn't weakness; it's courage in its rawest form."

Aarav stood up and said:
"To be
"It is the courage to say, "I'm hurting," when the world expects a smile."
"It is the honesty to admit, "I don't know," in a culture obsessed with certainty."
"It is the quiet bravery of showing your heart – even when it might be broken."

"My dear friends! Vulnerability is not about oversharing; it's about authenticity. It's when you let go of the need to appear perfect and choose instead to be present. When you allow yourself to feel – joy, pain, love, fear – you open the door to genuine connection."

"Strength built on denial is fragile. But strength rooted in vulnerability is unbreakable, because it comes from truth."

He looked around and began to speak:

"When you accept your own imperfections, you become more compassionate – not just toward yourself, but toward others. You begin to see that everyone is fighting unseen battles. You realize that connection is born not through perfection, but through shared humanity."

"To be vulnerable is to be alive."
"And to be alive – truly, fully, unapologetically – is the greatest strength there is."
"It takes courage to be seen as you truly are."

"We live in a world where people wear masks – not just during carnivals or festivals, but every single day. We wear smiles when our hearts are tired. We act strong when we feel fragile inside. We say "I'm fine" when we're breaking a little more every night."

Aarav raised his right hand and asked:
"But what if the real strength lies not in hiding your pain, but in being honest about it?"
"From a young age, we are told to be strong."
"Don't cry."
"Don't show weakness."
"Be brave."
"But no one tells us what true bravery looks like. Bravery is not about never crying – it's about daring to cry in front of someone and trusting that they will understand."
"It's not about being fearless – it's about walking forward despite the fear."
"The truth is – the strongest people you know are not the ones who never fall. They are the ones who fall, admit it, and still rise again."
"Remember (with clenched fist):"
"Every strong person you admire once felt weak."
"Every confident smile once hid fear."
"Every healed heart once broke open."
"So don't hide your pain – love it."
"Do not get away from your fear – honor it."

Aarav finished his speech, panting slightly, and sat down. There was silence in the class for a while, then there was a long round of applause.

Aarav wrote very enthusiastically in his diary:

"Today, I let myself be vulnerable. I shared my pain, my struggles... and instead of being judged, I felt understood. Maybe strength isn't about hiding or fighting alone—it's about opening up, even when it scares you."

He drew two figures, one reaching toward the other, connected by a faint line of light.

Below it, he added:
"5 days left."

He admired himself:
"Maybe being brave doesn't mean being unbroken. Maybe it means showing the cracks, letting the light in... and letting others see them too. Now, I felt that my struggles could coexist with connection, courage, and hope—vulnerability as a bridge rather than a weakness."

"Your purpose may be quiet now, but it is still alive."

Day 26 – A Glimpse of the Future

"Love begins the moment you believe you are worthy of it."

The morning sunlight streamed through Aarav's window, bright and unwavering. He felt a quiet energy stirring within him—a sense that life might hold something more than survival. This morning felt calm yet full of energy. The air was fresh, and the soft light of the sun made everything look peaceful. Aarav started his day with a quiet mind – no rush, no chaos. A glass of water, a few deep breaths, and a short walk helped him feel grounded.

The birds were chirping, the sky was clear, and there was a quiet confidence in the air. He could feel a sense of purpose growing within him – gentle but strong. It reminded him that every new morning is a small chance to reset, to move forward, and to do a little better than yesterday.

"Maybe... just maybe... the future isn't as dark as I thought," he whispered.

During a quiet walk in the park, Aarav sat on a bench and let his mind wander. He imagined finishing college with purpose, pursuing music again, perhaps even performing publicly someday. He pictured helping someone in the same way Rahul or the stray dog had touched him—sharing knowledge, kindness, and care.

The images were fragile, tentative, but they felt real. A faint smile tugged at his lips.

"What if... I could have a life that matters? That I choose, not just endure?" he murmured.

“It’s just daydreaming. It won’t happen.”

“Maybe. But even imagining it feels different. It feels... alive.”

“And what if I fail again?”

“Then I try again. Possibility is worth more than despair.”

Aarav had spent years trying to understand his pain—its causes, its purpose, its endless repetitions. But this morning, he realized that understanding pain was not enough; what mattered now was what he would do after it.

He had spent too long surviving. Now, he wanted to build.

He began writing down the things he wanted to do—not out of impulse, but out of clarity.

“Complete the degree I left unfinished.”

“Start the small design studio I always dreamt of.”

“Help students who feel lost, like I once did.” Each goal was born from a scar, but also from a lesson.

Pain had taught him endurance; now it would teach him discipline. He began to rebuild his activities. He replaced the habit of overthinking with a ten-minute walk before sunrise.

He started reading again—not to escape, but to learn. He promised himself one act of progress, no matter how small: a call, a draft, a new skill, a plan refined.

Eventually, he understood that healing is not waiting—it is doing.

Whenever doubts whispered—What if you fail again?—Aarav answered softly, Then I'll begin again, but stronger. He knew the road ahead would still be uneven, but he was no longer afraid of difficulty. Pain had already trained him for discomfort; now he would use that strength to create.

He started volunteering once a week at a local youth center. The first time he spoke to a boy who said, "I feel like I'll never be enough,"
Aarav saw his younger self. He didn't give advice that sounded polished or perfect. He simply said, "You don't have to be unbroken to move forward. You just have to begin." That moment lit something inside him—a purpose bigger than his own story.

Now, his day stopped revolving around what he had lost. It revolved around what he was building. His pain became energy; his mistakes became instruction. He stopped chasing happiness as an escape and began cultivating meaning as a habit.

When exhaustion set in, he still felt the old weight on his chest. But now, he knew how to stand beneath it. He would look at his journal—pages filled with ideas, schedules, half-written plans—and remind himself that progress isn't always visible, but it's always growing quietly beneath the surface.

He began sketching designs again, his creativity no longer fueled by frustration, but by curiosity. The more he worked, the less he thought about proving others wrong. The focus had shifted inward—to becoming the man he himself would be proud of.

Aarav no longer wanted to "move on" from pain; he wanted to move through it, carrying its wisdom forward. He began to see his future as a landscape he could shape—one project, one act of kindness, one quiet victory at a time.

He still had fears, but they no longer dictated his pace. He had plans—not perfect, not guaranteed—but real. His dreams were not grand illusions now; they were structured visions backed by effort.

As he looked ahead, Aarav realized that the most powerful future is not the one untouched by pain, but the one built beyond it. His life would not be defined by what hurt him, but by what he created after it.

He had finally stopped asking, "Why me?"
Now, he asked, "What next?"
And that single change of question became the turning point of his entire life.
Aarav took his diary and penned on a new page:
"Today, I allowed myself to see a future beyond pain. I pictured a life filled with music, purpose, and kindness. Maybe it's fragile, maybe uncertain... but it exists. And maybe noticing it is the first step toward building it."
"Maybe life isn't only about surviving. Maybe it's about creating, imagining, and moving toward something that feels meaningful... even if I take it one small step at a time."
He drew a faint sunrise behind a mountain—symbolizing hope rising above darkness.

Below it, he added:
"4 days left."

"You are worthy, even if you don't feel it yet."

Day 27 – Embracing Life

"Strength is built not in comfort, but in surviving storms."

The morning felt different today—warmer, more alive. Aarav woke with a subtle but undeniable sense that he wanted to participate in life, not just endure it.

"Maybe today... I can choose life, not just for tomorrow, but for me," he whispered.

Aarav decided to start small but meaningful. He organized his room, threw away things he no longer needed, and arranged his desk to be a space for creation and focus. Each action felt like reclaiming control over his life. Later, he returned to the park where he had fed the stray dog. This time, he carried water and food, smiling as the dog recognized him and wagged its tail.

"I'm here... I exist... I matter," he thought.
"It's just a few small actions. Why does it feel so significant?"
"Because each one is intentional. Each one says, 'I choose life.' That matters more than you think."
"I'm scared. What if tomorrow feels the same as before?"
"Then I'll choose again. Life is a series of choices. Today, I choose."

He remembered planting a sapling with his father at age nine. Every day he watered it, cared for it, and watched it grow. Life had taught him then: nurturing something—even small—creates growth and meaning.

"Maybe I can nurture my life the same way," he whispered.
Life was happening around him—and he was part of it.

Meera sat beside him, sketchbook closed, eyes bright.
"You seem... different," she said. "Happy, I mean."

"I am," Aarav replied softly. "I've learned something important: life is about tiny sparks, tiny steps, and sharing light. I've realized that even the smallest act—helping someone, noticing beauty—creates meaning."

She nodded. "You've grown so much. You're inspiring others without even realizing it."

Aarav smiled faintly. "Maybe that's the point. Life isn't just about surviving. It's about living... and helping others live too."
He closed his eyes, feeling the warmth of the sun on his face. The journey had been long, painful, and uncertain. But it had also been filled with small victories, sparks of joy, acts of courage, and growing connections.

For a while, they didn't talk. Aarav tossed a small pebble toward the pathway, missing a puddle by an inch.

Meera (moved to him and with smile): "You still think you don't do enough?"

He laughed softly. "Not as much as I used to. These days, I'm learning to just... let things be. Not everything needs to be fixed or figured out."

Meera: "That's growth, Aarav. Took me years to understand that. I used to fill every minute doing something – studying, planning, overthinking. Now, I actually enjoy sitting like this, watching people pass by."

She pointed to an old man walking his dog. "Look at him. He's been here every evening this week. Same bench, same time. He just sits and watches the world go by. Maybe he figured it out before we did."

Aarav smiled, following her gaze. "Maybe he has. Or maybe he's just enjoying the quiet. Sometimes, that's enough." There was another pause – comfortable this time. The kind that exists only between people who understand each other.

A leaf fell between them, spinning gently before landing on the bench. Aarav picked it up, tracing its veins. "I think I used to fear stillness. I thought if I stopped for even a moment, I'd be left behind. But lately, I've realized that the most beautiful things happen in stillness – sunsets, reflections, forgiveness."

Meera: "You ever think about how much we rush? Everyone's always chasing something – a job, money, validation, whatever. But when do we actually live?"

Aarav: "Yeah. I've been thinking about that too. When I was going through my worst phase, I kept asking 'why me?'. But now I think it was just life slowing me down – forcing me to look around."

Meera turned toward him. "You sound peaceful saying that. Earlier you would've sounded angry."

He chuckled. "I was angry. At everything. But I realized – pain doesn't mean life's unfair. It just means I'm alive. Everyone's fighting something. Once you accept that, you stop expecting perfection."

Meera: "Acceptance... that's a big word. I think that's what embracing life really means. Not pretending everything's fine, but still finding small reasons to smile."

Aarav nodded slowly. "Exactly. Like this evening. It's nothing special, but it feels... enough."

She looked at him and smiled. "Enough — that's a nice word. We never use it. We always say 'I want more', 'I need better'. But when you start saying 'this is enough', you start feeling lighter."

Aarav: "You're right. I think we spend half our lives running from silence. But maybe silence is what heals us."

Meera: "Hmm... yeah. Silence and people who don't make it awkward."

Aarav grinned. "So I make the cut?"

Meera laughed. "Barely. But yes."

They both laughed quietly, their laughter blending with the sound of the wind. The sky was now turning from orange to purple. A streetlight flickered on behind them.

Aarav: "You know, Meera... I think life is simpler than we make it. We just complicate it trying to control everything."

Meera: "True. We think we can plan happiness — but it sneaks up on you in moments like this. Sitting on an old bench, talking about nothing."

Aarav looked thoughtful. "Maybe that's what embracing life means — not chasing big moments, but noticing the small ones."

She smiled gently. "Like now?"

He nodded. "Exactly like now."

For a few minutes, they said nothing. The evening settled around them – the hum of insects, distant laughter, the soft crunch of gravel as people walked by. Meera leaned back, taking a deep breath.

Meera: "You know, Aarav... I think I used to be scared of growing up. But now I'm kind of looking forward to it. If it means more peace, more understanding... maybe it's not that bad."

Aarav smiled at her honesty. "I used to feel the same. But I guess growing up isn't about age – it's about learning to see beauty in ordinary days."

Meera: "And forgiving yourself for the messy ones."

He nodded. "Yeah. Especially those."

The wind picked up, and a few drops of water from the tree above fell on them. They laughed again.

Meera: "Looks like nature agrees."

Aarav: "Or it's telling us to stop talking so seriously."

They both laughed and got up, stretching a little. As they started walking down the path, the lights from the park glowed softly behind them.

Meera (smiling): "You know, Aarav, maybe we don't need to figure life out. Maybe we just need to live it – slowly, honestly."

Aarav: "Yeah. One quiet evening at a time."

And with that, they walked on – not searching for answers, not chasing anything – just being there, present, alive, and okay with it.

After returning in his room, Aarav wrote in his diary:

"Today, I made small choices that mattered. I cleaned, I cared, I talked to Meera so long, I gave life to little things around me. Each action reminded me that life can be embraced, not just endured. Choosing life is a decision I can make... again and again."

He drew a small sprouting plant beside the entry, symbolizing growth and care.

Below it, he added:
"3 days left."

Before sleeping, Aarav whispered quietly:
"Maybe life isn't always bright, and pain will visit. But I can still choose, still nurture, still exist... and that is enough reason to stay."

For the first time in this month, choosing life didn't feel like an obligation or a struggle—it felt like reclaiming a part of himself he thought he had lost.

"You stood in the storm today. That is strength."

Day 28 – Gratitude in Small Things

"Even broken pieces can form a beautiful mosaic."

Today's morning is different. Aarav woke with a quiet awareness, a subtle shift in his perception.
"Maybe today... I can see what I've been overlooking," he whispered.

As he walked to college, Aarav paused to watch a bird hop along the path, its tiny movements full of purpose. He noticed the crispness of the air, the gentle warmth of the sun on his skin, and the way leaves rustled in the breeze.
"I didn't notice these before... I was too busy drowning in my issues," he thought. "Maybe there's beauty all around me, if I just pay attention."
At college, a friend offered him a cup of tea without asking—just a small gesture of care. Aarav felt a warmth bloom inside him, realizing that kindness was everywhere, often unnoticed.
"These are tiny things. Do they really matter?"
"Yes. Small things shape life. Gratitude isn't grand—it's noticing what's already here."
"And if tomorrow is hard again?"
"Then I can still find a moment, a sound, a sight, a smile... something to be grateful for. That can anchor me."

He remembered lying on the grass as a child, staring at the clouds and imagining shapes and stories. He had felt infinite curiosity and awe. He realized that sense of wonder was still possible—waiting for him to notice again.

"Gratitude is remembering I can still feel wonder," he whispered.

Back in his room, Aarav opened his almirah and took his notebook to write his entire day feel in different way. He saw his daily diary but he put that in bed with soft smile and said: "Wait dear, will come to you at the end."

He opened a new page of the notebook and started writing-
"Tonight feels quieter than usual. The city outside hums faintly, like a distant memory, but here in my room, there's only the sound of my pen against paper."

"I don't know why, but I feel strangely content – not because something great happened, but because I suddenly see the beauty in the small things I used to ignore."

"Maybe that's what gratitude really is – not waiting for life to become perfect, but noticing that it already is, in its own imperfect way. The cup of tea beside me has long gone cold, yet its faint aroma still feels comforting. The soft light on my desk flickers, and instead of feeling annoyed, I feel thankful that I even have a light to sit under."

"All my life, I've chased bigger things – success, validation, the next goal. But today, I realized how much peace lives in the unnoticed moments. The warmth of the sun after days of rain. The laughter that suddenly breaks a heavy silence. The way someone says my name with care. These little things, they don't shout – they whisper, and we miss them unless we're still enough to listen."

"I think we forget too often that just being alive is a rare privilege. The heart beats on its own; the breath returns again and again without us asking. Maybe that's God's quiet way of reminding us that we are loved – even when we don't see it."

So tonight, I'm writing this to remember:
"Gratitude doesn't come from having everything."
"It comes from seeing the sacred in small things and realizing that life, just as it is, is enough."

He closed the notebook with gratitude and jumped into the bed to open his daily diary.

He drew a small sun with tiny stars around it, each representing a blessing.

Below it, he added:
"2 days left."

"Your breakdown is not the end—it is part of your success."

Day 29 – The Penultimate Choice

- An Array of Hope

"Despair is loud, but hope whispers steadily beneath it."

The morning was gray, the sky heavy with clouds. Aarav woke with a restless heart. Though the past days had brought sparks of hope, today felt different—a whisper of doubt, a shadow of the old despair he had struggled against for weeks.

"Tomorrow... the last day. And yet... I feel the old weight pressing again," he whispered.

On his way to college, Aarav passed the same bridge he had walked by during the earliest days of his despair. The thought flashed: "I could end this now... one final choice, one instant escape from pain."

His heart raced. The old spiral of hopelessness tried to convince him: "You've been struggling for days. Nothing will change. You're better off gone."

Aarav paused, hands gripping the railing, staring at the flowing river below. The familiar temptation clawed at his mind, sharp and insistent.

"It's easier... painless... final."

"Yes. But is it brave? Or just surrender disguised as relief?"

"What if I fail? What if the pain comes back anyway?"

"Then I have learned something—today is my choice, not yesterday's despair. And I can choose again tomorrow. That is strength."

"But the fear... it's overwhelming."

"Courage isn't absence of fear. Courage is choosing life despite fear. I've done it before. I can do it again."

He remembered the 28 days he had lived through—the small victories, the laughter, the acts of kindness, the rediscovery of dreams, the sparks of connection. Each memory reminded him: he had survived despair before; he had chosen life, even in darkness.

"If I end it now... I erase all the strength I've built," he whispered.

Aarav saw a boy in the park, approached him, hesitant. The boy's wheelchair was nimble, his smile bright as he delivered newspapers. Aarav's chest tightened; admiration and jealousy mingled.

"How can he be so happy... with so much less than I have?" he thought.

Aarav: "Hey... um... I see you're... really happy. How do you do it? I mean... you—you're limited... and yet..."

Boy: "Limited? I'm not limited—I just live differently. Why would I waste time complaining?"

Aarav felt a flicker of resentment. "Different? Easy for you to say when you don't even know what it feels like to be normal."

Aarav (bitterly): "Do you know how hard it is to feel trapped in your own mind? To wake up every day with nothing but despair?"

Boy (frowning): "And you think my body doesn't trap me? You think I don't face pain, struggle, and barriers every single day? Yet here I am, working, laughing, living!"

Aarav's jaw tightened. "Yeah, but at least you have purpose. You have... structure. I... I just feel empty inside."

Boy (leaning forward, voice sharp but calm): "Purpose isn't given. It's chosen. I choose it. You can choose yours too—but whining won't create it."

Aarav felt anger rise. "You think it's that simple? Just choose happiness? Just decide to be okay?"

Boy (smiling, though firm): "Not simple. Not easy. But necessary. Complaining doesn't fix life. Action does. Even if it's tiny steps."

Aarav (quietly, almost trembling): "I've tried... I've failed... so many times. Why should I even keep trying?"

Boy (pausing, then softly): "Because trying is the only proof you're alive. Look at me—I've fallen countless times, but I still get up. Not because life is fair, but because I can still choose to live. You have the same choice."

Aarav (angrily, but beginning to see truth): “Easy for you to say when your struggles are... visible. People see them, maybe even help you.”

Boy (firmly): “And you think invisible struggles are easier? Pain isn’t measured by what people notice. It’s measured by whether you give up or keep going. You’re stronger than you think—you just refuse to see it.”

Aarav looked down, shame and realization rising. “I... I guess I never thought about it that way.”

Boy (smiling warmly, gentle): “Good. Now think: today, you can take one step. One small thing. Make a choice. That’s how life starts to change.”

Aarav (nodding slowly, softening): “Maybe... maybe I can try. Even just one step.”

Boy: “That’s all it takes. One step. Then another. That’s hope.”

Aarav: “I envy you... not your challenges, but your courage. I want that.”

Boy (grinning): “Then take it. You have it inside you already. You just need to claim it.”

Aarav smiled faintly, the weight in his chest easing slightly.

"Maybe hope isn’t magic... maybe it’s choosing to see strength in yourself, even when it hurts," he thought.

They shook hands, and Aarav felt something shift—a spark of inspiration that was real, tangible, and his own.

The night felt heavier than usual. The clock on the wall ticked like a reminder — only one day left. Aarav sat on the edge of his bed, staring at nothing, his mind flickering between two worlds — the one he was living and the one he was about to leave.
Every breath carried a question, every silence echoed a confusion he could not escape. The idea of ending it all no longer scared him; it was the uncertainty of what if that tore him apart.

His thoughts swung like a pendulum — sometimes whispering "enough, just rest", and other times screaming "wait, what if tomorrow changes everything?" The weight of time pressed on his chest. He wondered if people would remember him, or if his absence would simply blend into the routine noise of life. There was no hatred left in him, no anger — only exhaustion, and a faint longing for peace.

Yet, deep within that fog of despair, something small refused to die — a faint, stubborn flicker. Maybe it was hope. Maybe it was fear. He couldn't tell anymore. But it kept him awake, made him question his decision even now, when the end seemed so close. Aarav realized that sometimes the hardest choice isn't between life and death — it's between giving up now and giving yourself one more chance.

As the night thinned into dawn, he whispered to himself, "Just one more day."
And even though the decision was near, that tiny whisper changed everything.

Aarav flipped the new page and wrote in his diary:

"Today, I met a boy my age who faces challenges I cannot imagine. We argued, we disagreed, I resented him for being stronger in ways I wasn't. But then he taught me the most important lesson: courage and hope aren't about what life gives you—they're about what you choose. I choose life. I choose hope."

"Today, I faced the final temptation of despair. The thought of escape was strong... but stronger was the life I've begun to build. Every small victory, every spark of hope, every connection matters. Choosing life is hard, but it is mine—and that is enough."

"Tomorrow will come. And I will meet it. Not as the boy who wanted to give up, but as someone who has learned to fight, to hope, and to choose life... one step at a time."

He drew a bridge above a flowing river, with footsteps moving forward—one step at a time.

Below it, he added:
"1 day left."
"only 1 day left."

"You heard the whisper today. Hold onto it."

Day 30 – The Final Confession

"Hope isn't the absence of pain-it's the courage to keep walking with it."

The morning light slipped gently through the curtains, scattering gold across Aarav's room. For the first time in weeks, he didn't turn away from it. The sun didn't sting his eyes—it felt warm, alive, forgiving. The air carried the smell of wet earth after a brief dawn drizzle, a quiet promise of renewal.

Aarav sat on the edge of his bed, fingers locked together, heart strangely calm. Twenty-nine days ago, he had made a dark decision—to end his story. But life, in its quiet persistence, had whispered back to him. Somewhere between sleepless nights and silent mornings, he had found a reason to stay.

Now came the hardest part—not survival, but confession. The thought of facing his parents filled him with shame. He wasn't afraid of their anger, but of their tears. How could he tell them he once chose death, and now wanted life? Still, he knew this morning wasn't about guilt—it was about truth. The same truth that had pulled him out of despair. The same truth that asked him to begin again.

He stood, took a deep breath, and let the light wash over his face. The world outside was waking, bright and hopeful. So was he. Today, he would speak—not of ending, but of beginning.

Aarav – embarrassed, nervous, and trembling slightly as he held his diary in his hands. It was his secret companion, the only place where he had poured his loneliness, his failures, his hidden cries. And tonight, he had decided – it was time to tell the truth.

His mother sat beside him, quiet and patient, sensing a storm inside him. His father stood near the door, his posture upright but his eyes soft, full of worry that he had been too afraid to voice.

Aarav's breath shook. "Mamma... Papa..."
He tried to speak, but his throat closed up. A tear rolled down before the words could.
His mother placed her hand over his. "Say it, my son," she whispered. "Whatever it is... just say it."

Aarav looked up – his lips quivering, his eyes red.
"Twenty-nine days ago..." he started, voice barely audible, "I almost... killed myself. I decided to commit sui....(swallowed air)....cide."

Sui...cide........Suicide, The words hung in the air like thunder.

His mother froze, her eyes widening as tears welled up instantly. His father's breath caught; his strong hands clenched into fists at his sides. He didn't move, didn't speak – but his face, usually calm and composed, broke.

Aarav continued, sobbing now. "I was tired, Mom... tired of pretending to be okay. Every morning felt heavy. I couldn't focus, couldn't smile, couldn't breathe without feeling like a burden. I thought maybe... if I disappeared, everything would be easier for everyone – for you, for Papa..."

He hid his face in his palms. "That night, I wrote my last letter. I was ready. But when I saw your photo on my table – you both, smiling together – I couldn't do it. I cried all night. I felt like a coward. Like a failure."
Tears streamed freely down his cheeks now.
"I didn't know how to tell you. I was scared, Papa... scared that you'd be angry."

There was silence.
Then, his mother's trembling voice: "Aarav... I knew this, my son."

Aarav looked up in disbelief. "You... knew?"

She nodded, her tears flowing now. "I found your diary. I read those pages. Every word cut through me, but I stayed quiet. Not because I didn't care – but because I wanted you to find your voice again. I wanted my son to come back on his own terms. I wanted to see you win against the darkness, against the despair."

Aarav collapsed into her arms, crying. "I'm so sorry, Mom..."

She held him tighter. "Don't be sorry, kid. You didn't lose. You survived. That's what matters."

For a long moment, only the sound of their breathing filled the room. Then – his father finally spoke. His voice was deep, steady, but there was a tremor of emotion he couldn't hide.
"Aarav," he said softly, taking a step forward, "look at me, champ."

Aarav hesitated, then lifted his head. His father's eyes – usually full of discipline and composure – were glistening. He knelt down in front of his son and placed a firm hand on his shoulder.

"I failed you," he said quietly.
Aarav's eyes widened. "No, Papa–"

"Yes," his father interrupted, his voice breaking. "I did. I was so busy trying to make you strong that I forgot to show you that it's okay to be weak sometimes. I thought silence meant strength. But now I see – you were screaming inside that silence."

His words hit deep.
"I read people all day in my work," his father continued, his voice trembling. "But I couldn't read my own son's pain. That's my failure, Aarav... not yours."

Aarav's tears fell faster. "Papa, please... don't say that. You were never wrong. I just... I didn't know how to talk."

His father took a long, shaky breath and then pulled him into his arms. For a few seconds, Aarav froze – and then he broke down, clutching his father tightly. It was the first time in months he had felt the warmth of his father's embrace.

"My son," his father whispered, his voice cracking, "I've seen battles in life – financial struggles, failures, sleepless nights – but none of them scared me like the thought of losing you. You're my pride, Aarav. You're my reason to fight every day."

Aarav sobbed against his chest. "I'm so sorry, Papa..."

His father shook his head, his hand on Aarav's back. "Don't ever apologize for feeling pain, son. Real strength isn't in hiding your wounds – it's in showing them and still choosing to live. You did that today. You came back to us."

Aarav's mother wiped her eyes, smiling through tears. "You see, Aarav? That's what we always wanted – not perfection, but you."

Aarav looked at both of them – his mother's tearful tenderness, his father's strong but broken gaze – and something changed inside him. His tears slowed. His breath steadied.

"Mamma, Papa..." he said softly, "I don't want to die anymore. I want to live. I want to write again – not about pain, but about what I've learned from it. I want to help others like me. Maybe through words, maybe through my story."

His father smiled faintly, pride flickering through his tears. "Then write, champ," he said firmly. "And never stop. Because your story will give hope to others. That's real success – not marks, not money – but saving a life through your own truth."

Aarav nodded, tears falling again – but this time, they were warm, not heavy. "You both are my strength. I wouldn't be here without you."

His mother kissed his forehead. "And we'll always be with you – in your strength and your weakness."

His father added quietly, "And whenever the darkness comes again, don't fight it alone. Talk to us. Promise?"

"I promise, Papa," Aarav whispered.

The three of them sat together – arms around each other – as the golden light faded and night filled the sky. But inside that room, something glowed brighter than before – the light of love, forgiveness, and new beginnings.

Aarav opened his diary, flipping past the old pages filled with pain, and turned to a fresh one.

At the top, he wrote in firm, hopeful letters:

"Day 1 – I choose to live."

His father placed a hand on his shoulder.

"Now," he said softly, "that's my son."

And for the first time in a long time, Aarav smiled – not the forced smile of survival, but the genuine smile of rebirth.

Aarav fully embraced life and discovers a renewed sense of purpose.

"You made it to Day 30."

"This is not the end of a countdown—it is the beginning of your new story because Life is not about avoiding pain, but discovering reasons worth living for."

"It's not Day 30 of Suicide.....It's Day 1 of Life"

A Dawn of New Life

"Every Life Has Some Reasons to Shine. Find Yours."

A New Beginning

Two weeks had passed since Aarav's confession.

The heaviness in his chest had started to lift – not because the pain had magically disappeared, but because he no longer carried it alone. Every morning felt a little lighter now. The diary on his desk no longer frightened him; it had become a canvas for hope.

His mother would often sit quietly beside him while he wrote, sometimes placing a cup of coffee by his side without a word. His father, though still the same reserved man on the outside, had changed too – he made time to simply be there. A hand on Aarav's shoulder as he studied, a quiet "How are you feeling?" before leaving for work, a long walk together after dinner. For Aarav, that presence spoke louder than any advice.

One evening, as Aarav sat with his diary, his father entered his room holding a printed flyer. "Aarav," he said, "look at this."

It was a small poster announcing a local youth meet-up on mental health and resilience, organized at the city library. "They're inviting young people to share their experiences," his father continued. "Would you... like to speak?"

Aarav hesitated. The old fear flickered for a second. Public speaking? Talking about his darkest days in front of strangers?

He glanced at his father, who was watching him quietly — no pressure, just patient eyes full of belief.
Aarav swallowed. "Papa... I don't know if I'm ready."

His father walked over and sat beside him. "You don't have to be perfect, champ. You just have to be honest. Do you know what true courage is?" Aarav shook his head.

His father smiled faintly. "True courage is when you turn your pain into someone else's hope. You survived. That makes you a living example. If even one boy or girl listens to you and steps back from the edge, that's a life saved. That's your power now."

Aarav felt something stir inside him. He thought of his diary — of those nights when he wished someone would tell him he wasn't alone. Maybe now... he could be that voice.

He took a deep breath. "Okay, Papa. I'll do it."

His father's eyes softened with pride. "That's my son."

The Day of the Speech

The city library's small auditorium was filled with young faces. Some looked curious, some nervous, some simply lost. The air smelled of books and coffee. Aarav stood backstage, clutching his diary like a lifeline.

His mother stood near the aisle, her hands folded, silently praying. His father was leaning against the back wall – his expression calm, but his eyes betraying the quiet pride of a man who had watched his son walk back from the edge.

When Aarav's name was called, he walked to the podium, his heart pounding. The microphone squeaked softly as he adjusted it.

He glanced at the audience – then at his parents. His mother gave him an encouraging nod. His father, without saying a word, lifted his hand slightly – a small gesture that said, I'm here. You're safe.

Aarav took a deep breath and began.
"forty-five days ago," he said, his voice trembling but clear, "I almost ended my life. I had decided to commit suicide."

A hush fell over the room. Everyone looked each other with anxiety. Everyone's mouths dropped open in surprise.

Aarav started confidently: "I thought I was alone. I thought I was weak. I thought my failures defined me. But I was wrong."

He opened his diary.
"This diary was once filled with my pain. 30 days of pain, despair, anxiety, spark, reasons, rejoice, resentment, tears, courage, hope and bla..bla...bla...Today, I've written something new. I want to read it to you."
He read aloud the first page:

'Day 1 – I choose to live.'
'Day 2 – I choose to speak.'
'Day 3 – I choose to help.'

He looked up at the audience. "I'm not here as someone who has it all figured out."

"I'm here as someone who is still healing. But I've learned this – silence doesn't save us. Talking does. Reaching out does. And sometimes, just one conversation can pull you back from the edge."

Somewhere in the crowd, a girl wiped her eyes. Another boy nodded silently.

Aarav's hands steadied on the podium.
"I'm living proof," he continued, "that darkness doesn't mean the end. You can walk through it. And if you're there now... please, talk to someone. Don't let it win. You matter. More than you know."

He closed the diary. His eyes found his father's across the hall. His father's lips curved in the smallest, proudest smile Aarav had ever seen.
When the applause began, it wasn't polite or restrained – it was warm, genuine, and long. Aarav felt his throat tighten, but this time, it was not from pain. It was from the realization that his voice had reached someone.
After the program, Aarav's father met him outside the hall. He didn't say much – just placed a hand on Aarav's shoulder and looked him straight in the eyes. "You did it, champ," he said softly. "You've already saved lives today."

Aarav smiled, tears in his eyes. "You were right, Papa. Real courage is turning pain into hope."

His father squeezed his shoulder, his voice thick. "And you've just become braver than any man I know."

His mother joined them, hugging Aarav tightly. "This is just the beginning, my dear."

Aarav looked at both of them – his anchors, his strength – and for the first time in a long time, the future didn't feel like a burden. It felt like a gift.

He opened his diary again and wrote:

"Day 15 — I choose to be someone's reason to live."

His father glanced at the page and smiled. "And we choose," he said quietly, "to stand beside you always."

Together, they walked out of the library — into the evening light. The world was still the same, but Aarav was not.

He had not just survived..!

He had begun to live.........!!

The story of your survival may become the reason someone else chooses life."

"Make your story - A Story of Courage, Resilience, and Choosing Life."

Your Story

"There is no greater agony than bearing an untold story inside you. So pen down your agony, if any, you have."

"A word after a word after a word is power"

About the author

Dr. Pankaj Srivastava is a surgeon by profession and a writer by passion – a craftsman who heals with precision – yet his heart beats to the rhythm of words. A seeker of meaning in both science and silence, he finds his refuge in Hindi, English, and Urdu literature. He has explored the art of expression beyond the boundaries of medicine.

Founder of Shivoham Publications in Varanasi, Dr. Pankaj envisions literature as a sacred dialogue between the soul and the universe. His creative journey flows parallel to his medical calling – one mends the body, the other heals the unseen wounds of existence.

Dr. Pankaj has published numerous research papers in reputed international medical journals, reflecting his academic excellence. Alongside his medical pursuits, he has edited and published two acclaimed literary works in Hindi Poetry – "Unmukt Muktak" and "Sakalya" – which showcase his sensitivity towards human emotions and life's deeper philosophies. Each of the book is echoing his reflective spirit and spiritual depth.

Through his writings, Dr. Pankaj bridges the distance between life and death, reason and emotion, the seen and the felt – reminding us that every choice, like every heartbeat, matters.

His writings mirror the intricate blend of science and soul, discipline and imagination – a rare confluence that defines both his profession and his prose.

www.ingramcontent.com/pod-product-compliance
Lightning Source LLC
Chambersburg PA
CBHW011802160726
48282CB00035B/1236
* 9 7 8 8 1 9 8 2 6 1 9 3 9 *